"I adored this book! Like, I seriously hugged it when I was done. This is quintessential middle grade—charming, funny, real, and overflowing with heart."

—Olugbemisola Rhuday-Perkovich, author of
8th Grade Superzero, *Two Naomis*, and *Naomis Too*

"This book is my favorite combination of heartfelt and hilarious. Yumi Chung is a headliner!"   —Remy Lai, author of *Pie in the Sky*

"This book is hilarious."

—Sarah True, Joseph-Beth Booksellers (Cincinnati, OH)

"One of the best middle grade books I have read all year!"

—Robyn Broderick, The Reading Bug (San Carlos, CA)

"Yumi is a smart and sassy heroine, and *Stand Up, Yumi Chung!* is a poignant and charming story that appeals to the dreamer in all of us."

—Jackie Jou, Mysterious Galaxy Bookstore (San Diego, CA)

"This book made me cry, cheer, and laugh out loud."

—Bethany Strout, Tattered Cover Book Store (Denver, CO)

STAND UP, Yumi Chung!

Jessica Kim

Kokila

KOKILA

An imprint of Penguin Random House LLC, New York

Copyright © 2020 by Jessica Kim

Visit us online at penguinrandomhouse.com

Library of Congress Cataloging-in-Publication Data is available.
Printed in the United States of America
ISBN 9780525554974

3 5 7 9 10 8 6 4 2

Design by Jasmin Rubero
Text set in Stone Informal ITC Pro

To Phil, Olivia, and Lily

CHAPTER 1

I should have known better than to think anyone would listen to me at the Korean beauty salon.

"You want the perm?" asks the stylist in leather pants, running her fingers through my limp hair.

"Uh, I—I was thinking," I sputter, showing her my phone, "maybe you could give me something like this instead?"

After scrolling through Pinterest for "hairstyle makeover" all week, I've settled on this sleek pixie cut. It's definitely shorter than anything I've ever had before, but maybe that's exactly what I need before seventh grade starts next month. A change. Something bold for the New Me.

Mom emerges from the dressing room in a shiny black robe and plucks the phone from my hands in one swift motion.

"Yumi, no." She raises a generously penciled-in eyebrow. "Too short. You will look like a boy from BTS!"

"Mom!" I grab my phone back, ignoring the three robed aunties (who aren't really my aunties) laughing in the chairs next to me. "This is a really popular hairstyle these days."

"Let me see." My stylist's leather pants squeak as she bends over for a closer look. "No good. Your cheeks are too big for this cut."

I examine the picture again, noticing the model's sunken cheeks for the first time. I steal a glance at myself in the mirror, subtly sucking in my face.

Leather Pants scrunches my hair in her hands. "You need more volume." She combs my hair forward, obscuring the sides of my face. "Covers your yeodeureum."

My Korean isn't that fluent, but I know she's talking about my acne.

"She is right," Mom says.

My stomach twists. "Yeah, but I—I don't know. That's not the look I'm—"

Without letting me finish, Leather Pants turns to Mom. "Perm?"

"Yes, much better for her." She nods her chin to confirm and spins her chair to join the gaggle of gossiping aunties. Before I can object, they're back to swapping intel.

"Did you hear that Kim moksa-nim from Hosanna Baptist is sending his son to Cornell?"

"How about his other son? Tall lawyer?" Mom gives them a knowing glance. "He's same age as my older daughter."

Oh brother, not this again.

Meanwhile, a sharp chemical odor stings my nostrils as strands of my hair are twirled around spools attached to a giant octopus-like machine.

So this is what disappointment smells like. Another perm. So much for the New Me.

When my hair is completely rolled up, the perm machine and I are sent to the ventilated lounge for a half hour to marinate. Good thing I brought my new Super-Secret Comedy Notebook. I take it out from my bag and jot down something I've been thinking about.

It's really frustrating that my parents compare me to their friends' kids.

It's always "Why can't you play piano like Grace?" or "Why can't you speak Korean better like Joon?"

The other day they were telling me, "Did you know that Minji got into Harvard?"

I said, "Mom, give me a break. I'm only eleven years old!"

Then she tells me, "Minji is nine!"

Mom approaches, her head covered in enough aluminum foil to transmit radio waves to Mars. I immediately shove my notebook into my bag before she can scold me for "wasting time with that comedy nonsense."

She scoots the magazines off the chair next to me and sits. "Yumi, I have to tell you something very important."

I freeze. "About what?"

She picks up her steaming cup of barley tea with both hands. "You know," she says carefully, "business is not so good at restaurant right now."

"Uh-huh." This is not news. It's pretty much all my parents talk about these days. Ever since the new luxury high-rise condos went up all over Koreatown, foot traffic into our family's Korean barbecue restaurant has all but stopped. Dad blames the new people for hogging all the parking spots, driving up the rent, not supporting small businesses, and probably even causing global warming.

She blows softly into the celadon teacup, her fingers curled around it. "Yesterday I went to your school to talk to Mr. Beasley."

I stiffen at the mention of Winston Preparatory Academy's most crotchety administrator. "Why?"

She draws close and whispers, "To tell him we cannot afford to pay tuition next year."

"Wait. I don't have to go to Winston anymore?" A tightness I didn't even know I was holding in my shoulders magically lifts, and a giant grin spreads across my face. I consider the implications: no more starchy uniforms, no more Latin class, no more snotty cliques, and no more disappointed teachers.

FREEDOM!

I get a sudden urge to bust out my robot dance moves all over the salon. Not that I'd actually ever do that. Not while anyone was watching, anyway.

Instead I let out a satisfied sigh.

Going to a new school won't be easy, but at least it'll be a fresh start. A do-over of sorts. Maybe this time my yearbook will be signed by someone other than my teachers.

But then Mom shakes her head, the tin-foiled flaps rattling. "No, you still go to Winston." Instantly, my elaborate visions of the New Me skitter away into thin air.

I tug at a roller on my head that's wound too tightly. "But you just said we can't afford—"

She shushes me violently like I let it slip that she sometimes cooks with MSG.

"No, listen. Mr. Beasley says if you score at least ninety-eighth percent on exam, you can get the academic scholarship. Attend Winston. For free," she says, emphasizing the words *for free*.

"Huh? What exam?"

She scoots her chair closer to mine and pulls up an email on her phone. "Test is called SSAT. Secondary School Admission Test. You take the test on August sixteenth."

"WHAT?" My neck swings so fast I nearly unplug the giant perm machine. "Mom, that's in, like, two weeks. I can't—there's no way I can—"

Has the hair dye fried her brains? Does she actually expect me to ace a test I've never heard of like it's no big deal?

She clucks her tongue in disbelief. "You can attend best private school in Los Angeles. For free." She blinks long and hard. "Mommy and Daddy work so hard so you can have opportunities like this. You must do it."

This is Mom's go-to move for guilting me into doing something I don't want to do. Whenever she senses even an ounce of resistance, she busts out with, "We came here from Seoul to work seven days a week, sacrificed everything. Why? For you! So you can (insert undesirable thing here)." Play piano, go to Korean school, learn tae kwon do. It's like baking soda, useful in so many different scenarios. I'm dying to know what nonimmigrant parents say to coerce their kids.

Just then, Leather Pants pops in to check on us. She pokes around my scalp with the pointy end of a comb and readjusts the dials on the machine. "Everything okay?"

"Yes," I tell her, despite my nerves shooting through the roof.

She leads us to the main room of the salon.

Mom straightens her robe. "Yumi, if you study very hard and graduate with good grades from Winston, you can go to top university *like your sister*," she says, this time loud enough for the aunties to hear.

Ugh.

Leave it to Mom to steer this back to my sister and

her million and one academic achievements. As if they have anything to do with me. Hello, Yuri is literally a genius. An actual card-carrying member of Mensa with an IQ of 155. And I'm . . . just me. But that doesn't stop my parents from holding me to her impossible standard to "inspire me." It's the most unfair thing ever.

"But I can't—I'm not—" My scalp is burning. I can't tell if it's the chemicals or Mom getting under my skin.

Her posture softens, and she pats my knee. "Do not worry. I signed you up for hagwon to help you prepare for test."

I recoil. Not hagwon! The last place I want to be on my summer break is in a classroom. My head feels like when the computer mouse arrow turns into the spinning rainbow wheel. "But—but I don't want to—"

"Studying at hagwon is better than wasting time watching YouTube jokester all day."

"Jokester?" My breath catches in my throat. "Mom, Jasmine Jasper is *not* a jokester."

She's only the creator of the most hilarious kids' comedy tutorials on YouTube. Not to mention my personal hero.

"Too much screen time. Rots brain. You need to study."
She pulls down the hair-dryer dome over her head.

The dryer roars to life when she flips the switch, drowning me out completely.

Thanks, Mom, for flushing what's left of my summer vacation down the toilet.

Swirling, swirling, swirling. FLUSH.

The perm machine emits a series of earsplitting beeps, and Leather Pants scuttles back to take out my rollers. When she's done, she sprays some fruity-smelling product on my hair and gives it another scrunch-scrunch.

"You like?" She twirls my chair around so I'm facing the mirror.

I run my fingers through the still-wet ringlets on my shoulders, vexed. "It's . . . just like it was before," I tell her with a forced smile.

My hair looks like Top Ramen noodles, but I don't say anything.

Why bother? No one listens to me, anyway.

CHAPTER 2

The moment the restaurant door opens, I'm met with the familiar hum of activity and the aroma of just-grilled meat.

I wave my hand to clear the haze that lingers in the air, but it's no use. Barbecue smoke is no joke. Our restaurant is the only one in town that still uses charcoal grills. Even though everyone else has switched to the cleaner gas or electric ones, Dad refuses to change. He's convinced real charcoal imparts the most "traditional" taste. Which is why my clothes, no matter how many times I wash them, smell like a campfire. It's also earned me the nickname Yu-meat. Yep, because every sixth grader at Winston Academy dreams of being known as the-new-girl-who-smells-like-barbecue. I'll never forgive Tommy Molina for starting that.

"Go help your dad in the kitchen," Mom says, tying

on her apron, the straps bedazzled with rhinestones. "We have a short staff today for lunch rush."

"Okay, let me check my email first." That, and Jasmine Jasper's new vlog is supposed to be up today.

She shoots me a knowing glance. "Don't spend too much time on the computer."

"Five minutes, I promise."

Our restaurant office doubles as our living room away from home. It's got a couch, coffee table, computer, even a shiatsu foot massager. We probably spend more time here than in our living room at home.

I'm surprised to find my big sister behind the computer.

"Hey, Yooms," she says to me.

"Yuri!" I wrap my arms around her in a bonecrushing hug.

I haven't seen her as much since she moved across town for medical school last fall. Before then, I could count on catching her at the restaurant or at home taking care of me. She's always been like my third "cool" parent. The house and restaurant have felt so empty without her.

"What are you doing here?"

"Dad needed some technical assistance with the computer. He wants me to add an online reservation option to the website."

"Why? It's not like it's hard to get a table here."

She shrugs. "You know how Dad gets with his big ideas."

I glance at the wall of indecipherable code on the monitor. "Wow, that's pretty intense."

"You're telling me. All this needs to be updated. I was supposed to leave an hour ago." She glances at my hair. "Cute perm, by the way."

I scrunch my nose, remembering the atrocity atop my head. "Don't lie. I look like a wet poodle." I run my fingers through my spiral strands, but it only makes it frizz up some more. "Just watch, Tommy Molina is going to have a field day coming up with nasty names for me when school starts." Between Yu-meat, Wet Poodle, and Top Ramen, he's got enough material for a Netflix special.

"Don't let that little punk get under your skin." She tousles my hair. "Besides, it'll loosen up before then."

"It better." I sit on the edge of the desk. "Actually,

it'd be better if I never have to go back to Winston ever again."

"Aw, Yumi." My sister squeezes my wrist. "Maybe this year will be different. Maybe you'll make some new friends?"

"Mm-hmm." Not likely. Long before I transferred in, everyone at my fancy private school had already settled into impenetrable cliques of friends they've known since kindergarten. Not that I'd be included even if I were around back then. Hearing them talk about the stuff they do together on weekends at the country club makes me feel like we're from different planets. Like the time Alexis and Avery were gushing about an equestrian competition, and I jumped in with *Quest! I love that board game!* I didn't win many popularity points with that one. I've concluded that I'm better off keeping my mouth shut instead of trying to fit in where I don't belong. It's just easier.

Yuri smooths my hair. "You never know. New year. New possibilities."

"New bullies."

She laughs. "Just be yourself, and everything will come together on its own."

If only it could be that simple.

Right then, Dad pops his head into the room. "How's website? Is it working?"

"Almost done." Yuri clicks through the screens. "I just have to add one more plug-in."

"Good," he says, watching my sister code. "This is what we need to bring in the customers."

Doubtful. It's going to take a whole lot more than a dinky online reservation button for that to happen, but I don't want to burst his bubble.

Dad turns to me. "Yumi, I need your help. Bring the ban-chan to table three. We are getting the slam." The slam. That's Dad's rendition of the phrase *we're getting slammed.*

"Sure." I guess Jasmine's vlog will have to wait until later.

"Can you help? After you finish with website?" he asks Yuri. "Until end of service?"

"Yes," Yuri says without looking up, her fingers flying across the keyboard.

When I walk into the kitchen, Manuel, our restaurant's main cook, greets me with a big smile. "Someone got her hair done! You look great, cipota."

"Really? I feel like I'm five years old," I groan, pulling on my apron. "How am I supposed to go to middle school with *this*?" I fluff the sides of the frizzy cloud that is now my hair.

"If anyone gives you trouble about your hair"—he flexes his muscles—"show them your guns. Let them know that they can't mess with you."

"Yeah, right." I snort as I wash my hands in the sink. For the ten years Manuel's been working here, he's always said stuff like that. It's really silly, but if I'm being honest, it's nice to have someone who encourages you to stand up for yourself. In my case, it's the Salvadoran head cook from my parents' restaurant.

I open the lid of one of the pots on the stove and take a big whiff. "Smells great."

"You know, it's just a little sundubu, kimchi-jjigae, seolleongtang, and two orders of my famous doenjang-jjigae," he says, with a better Korean accent than mine.

"Mmmmmm. Mashigeta!" It truly looks delicious. Manuel can cook anything. His pupusas are just as legendary as the Korean dishes Mom taught him.

"You know it." He tosses soft tofu into the bubbly red

stew and gives it a sprinkle of fresh green onion for garnish before sending it out to the pass.

"How did your granddaughter's birthday party go the other day?" I ask him.

"Good. Sofia wanted something low-key, so we ended up having some people over for Pollo Campero and cake. A Little Mermaid one. It was chill."

Something pops into my head. "Oooh! That reminds me of a joke."

"Let's hear it."

"How are parents like broken refrigerators?"

"I give up. How?"

"They're loud, inconsistent, and have no chill!" I say, barely containing my giggles.

Manuel lets loose the best kind of whole-body laugh. "No chill!" He throws his head back and holds his belly with both hands. "Burn!"

"Thanks." He's one of the few people I feel comfortable telling my jokes to, because he's always honest with his feedback.

"Don't be too hard on your mom and pops, though. They're coming from a good place." He's still laughing as he piles the tiny side dishes of cubed radish, sesame bean sprouts, black beans, and marinated spinach onto a giant platter. "Listen, you better get this banchan out there before the customers start complaining."

"Right." I haul the platter up onto my shoulder and balance it the best I can. "I got this." I flex my biceps, which is about as thick as a chopstick.

"Atta girl!" He chuckles, flexing his arm right back at me.

"Keep working on those jokes, Yumi!" he shouts before going back to tend to the five pots of soup boiling on the stove.

I'm heading out to the dining area when Yuri pops out from behind the faded embroidered folding screen carrying two water pitchers.

Mom is already at table three greeting the bespectacled middle-aged man sitting with his family.

"How are you, Mr. Lee?" She collects the clunky leather-bound menus from the table. "Mrs. Lee, did you change your hair? This color looks so stylish on you! Samuel, I hear that you got first chair in your orchestra! Congratulations!"

After being in business at the same location for fifteen years, Mom knows all the regulars by name. Somehow she also remembers their favorite entrees, preferred spice levels, tipping patterns, and if they happen to have any eligible bachelors in the family. These days, the Lee family and a small handful of other loyal diners are the only people I ever see at our restaurant.

"You remember our daughters." Mom rests her hands on Yuri's shoulders. "Girls, insa to our guests."

"Annyeonghaseyo." We greet them with our heads bowed.

Mr. Lee sets his spoon down. "They are more beautiful each time we see them."

"Beauty is not everything." Mom clucks her tongue and loud-whispers to Mrs. Lee, "I'm afraid Yuri will never get married." She tosses her head with disdain. "She still has no boyfriend."

Yuri's porcelain skin flushes bright pink. You'd think we'd have grown immune to this stuff by now, but nope, it's still mortifying each time.

Mrs. Lee chuckles. "Mrs. Chung, your daughter is still a student. Why are you worried already?"

A faux-concerned expression cloaks Mom's face. "She cannot meet any nice boys because she always studying, studying, studying." Mom sighs dramatically, clutching the pendant hanging from her necklace. "So difficult to be youngest student at the UCLA medical school."

Mrs. Lee's spoon clinks, hitting the side of the dolsot bowl.

"Medical school already? I thought she was in high school," she says, like Yuri isn't standing right there.

Mr. Lee grunts. "Looks like teenager!"

Dad dashes over, nearly knocking the traditional wooden masks from the wall. He must have sensed there was a brag session going on.

"Mr. Lee, Yuri is not teenager anymore!" He pauses. "She is twenty years old. Skipped two grades and graduated from the university early," he adds, injecting himself into the conversation. I swear, my sister is like his own living, breathing trophy.

Mr. Lee indulges Dad. "Wah! So smart! She finished her studies two years early."

Dad swats at the air, feigning modesty, like they're talking about him.

"Did you hear that, son?" Mrs. Lee elbows her teenage son.

Yuri's face is now redder than the raw meat on the grill.

The boy looks up through his long bangs. "What?"

Wait for it.

"If you study hard like her, you can be a success, too," Mr. Lee says.

Ha! If I had a dollar for every time my parents told me that, I'd be able to buy our family a second restaurant.

Then Mom gestures to me. "And you remember our second daughter, Yumi."

Ack, they're all looking at me! I grab the pitcher and top off the already-full water cups on the table, trying hard to ignore Mrs. Lee's eyes roaming up and down, evaluating my every molecule. She squints, probably struggling to come up with a compliment.

"Your younger daughter is so . . . tall."

Sad. That's the best thing she can come up with. I'm not even that tall. I grab the metal tongs and flip the meat on the grill, avoiding all eye contact, hoping they'll change the subject.

"You know, our Yumi is so shy and quiet. We don't know what to do with her. She did not even tell us when she won the academic scholarship to Winston Academy in Beverly Hills," Mom says unblinkingly.

I nearly give myself whiplash. Mom. What. The. Heck.

She smiles at them with her fake no-teeth grin, willfully ignoring my silent outrage.

Yuri snickers behind me.

My mother has been known to stretch the truth to make us look good. Like the time she complained to everyone at the restaurant about how difficult it was to find a costume after I was handpicked to sing the solo in my first-grade Christmas pageant. "She sings like an angel, just like her father," she told everyone. In truth, I was assigned the humble role of Wiseman #2, with no speaking parts whatsoever, much less a solo.

"You are blessed. Two obedient and smart daughters. My son here is so lazy. He never studies. All he ever wants to do is play his violin." Mr. Lee knocks his knuckles on his son's scalp. "Last week, he told me he needs money to fly to New York to perform with his orchestra. Carnegie Hall or something. I tell him, what about your studies?"

So it begins. For the next good while, they go back and forth one-upping each other with their humble-brags.

Someone get me a barf bag.

If only my parents were proud of me for the things I can actually do.

CHAPTER 3

Later that night, I'm practicing new stand-up in front of my laptop.

In today's vlog, Jasmine Jasper swore that watching and critiquing video footage of yourself is the best way to improve stage presence. So that's what I'm doing. Normally, I'd rather eat saeu-jeot by the spoonful than watch myself on tape, but hey, if that's what the pro says, that's what the pro says. I'll do just about anything that'll help me become even a fraction as funny as she is.

I became a Jasmine Jasper fan when Yuri showed me her videos to cheer me up when I didn't get invited to my so-called friend's birthday party. I'll never forget Jasmine's stand-up about how she got her period during a sleepover but couldn't muster the courage to ask her friend's mom for a maxi pad because #shygirlproblems. She resorted to making makeshift pads out of folded toilet paper, but when they were playing Twister, it fell out of her shorts and the dog got ahold of it and went to town. For the rest of the night, Bella the beagle wouldn't stop sniffing her crotch for more.

Jasmine Jasper had me howling with her facial expressions, voice impersonations, plus the doggy sniffing sounds. It was the best distraction to help me forget how bummed I was about being left out of the party. Also, it was nice to know I'm not the only one who gets awkward in certain social situations. In some ways, I feel like Jasmine Jasper gets me, maybe more than anyone else in my life. And she's so fricking funny, too.

I wonder how many times she had to practice that maxi-pad bit in front of the mirror holding a hairbrush for a microphone before it was perfected. On her vlogs, she's always talking about the importance of challenging yourself to do things that make you uncomfortable. And how we can't ever improve until we put ourselves out there and practice, practice, practice.

If it worked for her, maybe it'll work for me, too.

Here goes nothing.

I uncap my pen, then tap the Play button, unfreezing my likeness on the screen. And instantly, it's beyond brutal.

Cringe. Cringe. Cringe.

Do I really sound like that? Do I really stand like that?

I force myself to get through the entire four minutes and twelve seconds of the clip, jotting down the million things I need to work on:

-talk way louder, slower

-stand up straight, posture too slouchy

-walk around more—you are not a plant

-stop saying "um"

-don't need to grip hairbrush with both hands

-no nervous giggling

-pause between jokes

-don't rush the delivery

-need more hand gestures to animate story

I flip back in my notebook to fix my dumpster fire of a bit. I reread it, and honestly, it's not the material. There's actually a lot of good stuff here. The real problem is my delivery. I'm totally uncomfortable, and it shows. My nervous tics are choking the humor out of my jokes.

But how am I supposed to stop acting nervous when I *am* nervous?

Hopeless, I fall onto my bed face-first. What I really need is a personality transplant. From a really spontaneous, naturally outgoing, fun-loving donor.

I picture waking up from surgery after having charisma and confidence stitched alongside my organs and being miraculously healed from my stifling self-consciousness. I'd leave the hospital a totally different person. I'd participate in class, have a ton of friends, and my jokes would land.

I'd turn into the person I've always wanted to be. I'd be the New Me!

I imagine the way the New Me would perform my act. The pen in my hand can't keep up with my ideas.

I'm convinced my hair is mad at me.

For years [note: emphasize this], my mom has insisted that I condition it, spray it, pomade it, and perm it to "give it the volume." That's a lot of product, and it's given me a severe case of dandruff. [point to crown of head] Look at this! It's like the Swiss Alps up there. You know what I think? I think that's my hair follicles . . . [whisper this loudly into the mic] getting revenge on me. I tried to tell my mom, "See! It's because of all the stuff you make me use." She looked at me sternly and said, "Not my fault you did not use enough."

Whatever. [shrug] Sometimes you just have to brush it off.

The comments and the dandruff.

Be careful how you treat your hair, friends. Next time you're in the bathroom, watch your back. [pause] No, I mean literally check it out with some mirrors or something [pantomime this]. You might have missed some flakes back there.

This will get me to loosen up. But can I really pull it off?

Jasmine Jasper says that sometimes you have to "fake it till you make it."

It's worth a try.

I adjust the laptop screen, stand up straight, and clear my throat. "All right, here it goes. Hair Bit: Take Two," I say into the camera.

I grip my hairbrush/microphone and project nice and loud. "I'm convinced my hair is mad at me—"

I glance at my notebook for the next line, but then a freaky face appears behind me on the laptop screen.

"AHHHHHHHHHHHHHH!"

I whip around to meet my fate.

Thankfully, it's just Mom, looking like a killer from a bad slasher movie in her Korean sheet mask.

"I bring you a study snack," she sings, carrying in a plate of sliced Asian pears. Our family's shih tzu, Nabi, follows behind her.

"Mom, you scared the shin kimchi out of me!" I say, holding my chest.

"Sorry." Mom points to the white cotton film slathered on her face with floral-scented goo. "I got the new facial mask. Secret ingredient is snail secretion. Helps with shrinking the pores."

Snail secretions? How did they even extract that? Images of snails on treadmills made of sponge fill my mind.

"You should try, too. Maybe help with your skin." Nabi jumps into her lap and licks Mom's snail-slimy chin.

I turn away. "No, I'm good." I'll keep my pimples, thanks.

She hands me a tiny fork from the plate. "Eat. I cut for you. Fruit is good for concentration," she says, trying not to move her mouth muscles.

By compulsion, Mom automatically starts tidying the stray papers and books on my desk. "How many times I have to tell you? You need to keep your room organized," she nags.

"Why does it bother you so much? I know exactly where everything is."

"Having nice-looking desk will bring peace and good energy. Just like having nice-looking skin and hair. You have to take care of outside to take care of inside."

She sweeps my bangs out of my face.

"If you say so, Mom."

She glances at my computer screen. "Are you still working on quadratic formula?"

I close my laptop and clutch it to my chest.

"No, I was just, uh, working on some other stuff."

"What kind of stuff?"

"Nothing . . . just some jokes." I set it on the desk.

Mom's creepy mask pinches in the middle with dissatisfaction. "Jokes? What for?" She tugs at the edges of the sheet to readjust it.

"For fun."

Can't a girl videotape herself practicing her stand-up act to a pretend audience for no particular reason without getting the third degree?

"Humph. Waste of time." Mom takes a seat on the edge of my polka-dot bedspread and rearranges my pillows by size. "Have you heard from Yuri?"

Nabi's curled tail wags at the sound of my sister's name.

"Not since I saw her at the restaurant earlier." I sprawl on the other end of my bed, staring at my closet door, where my K-pop posters hang next to my old Pokémon ones. "Why?"

She draws her mummy-wrapped face close to mine. "Did she mention she is spending time with any new . . . friends?" Mom looks at me like I should understand what she's getting at, but I don't have a clue where she's going with this.

"She's not answering my phone calls. Very unusual

for her." She nibbles on a sliver of pear through her mask.

I shrug. "She's probably hanging out with people from class."

"I knew it."

"Knew what?"

Her smug smile pulls the sides of the sheet mask, making her look like a lackluster Mexican luchador. "She has a boyfriend."

I bolt upright, startling Nabi. "Why would you think that?" Wow. Mom *is* one to jump to conclusions, but this is a stretch, even for her.

"Makes sense. She is so busy. Distracted. Hurry to go back to her apartment. Missing calls. She must be seeing someone special."

I roll my eyes. "Oh geez, Mom. Or she's just enjoying her freedom and living her best life."

At least that's what I'd be doing if it were my first time living outside my parents' house.

Mom disregards me. "I wonder if he is Korean. Maybe a medical student like your sister." She chews her fruit thoughtfully. "I need to find out if the aunties heard anything. Tell me any new information if she tells you, okay?"

"Sure." There's no use trying to convince a woman who won't be convinced, so I just roll with it. I figure, the sooner I agree, the sooner she'll go back to her room, and the sooner I can get back to practicing my hair salon bit.

Mom heads to the door with Nabi on her heels. "Okay, don't stay up too late. Tomorrow you start hagwon."

I almost forgot.

I flop back on my bed, burying my head under my pillow.

I'd rather be a snail chained to a sponge treadmill than go to hagwon.

CHAPTER 4

It's only my second day since I started my test-prep course, and I don't know how much more of this I can take. To no one's surprise, my parents enrolled me in Koreatown's most rigorous hagwon, which is run by Mrs. Pak, otherwise known as "Pak Attack" for her ability to whip kids into straight-A shape. But even the threat of her wrath can't compete with the lulling effect of the stuffy midday heat and the drone of the useless ceiling fan whirring overhead. I'm fighting just to keep my eyes open. If scientists ever wanted to explore ways to tranquilize animals without drugs, they should bring them here. They'd drop like flies in record time. Guaranteed.

I let out a defeated yawn. I better get used to this, since I'll be here three hours a day, five days a week for the rest of the summer. If I survive that long, that is.

What kind of parent would sign their child up for this? Judging by the line of cars dropping off kids at Mrs. Pak's hagwon every morning at nine, a buttload of Asian parents.

Clack. Clack. Clack. Clack.

I can tell from the clipped sound of Mrs. Pak's tassel loafers across the tiled floor that I'm in for it. I jolt back to life as I quickly scoot my Super-Secret Comedy Notebook back under my algebra worksheets and shuffle to find the right page.

Mrs. Pak paces in front of the whiteboard. Her head swivels, scanning the class for her next victim, her hands planted on her hips. "Who knows the answer?" she asks, but it's clear she's actually looking for the kid who doesn't.

Clack. Clack. Clack.

"Yumi."

Of course she settles on me. Dang, this lady has excellent intuition. Sweat prickles down my back under my T-shirt, and I still don't know which number we're on. "Uhhh." I gulp, panicked. I take a shot in the dark. "I-is it A?"

She sighs slow and long, like she's a deflating beach ball. "Try again," she says, daring me to get it right.

I fiddle with the staple that's struggling to hold together my giant packet. I look at my paper, but the jumble of numbers and variables does me no favors.

Ginny, an old elementary school friend I reconnected with here at hagwon, turns around and mouths something, but I can't quite make it out. Is she saying B, C, or D? They all look the same.

I go with my gut. "C?" I croak. My throat is like sandpaper.

Ginny smacks her forehead.

"Have you been paying attention?" Mrs. Pak snarls at me like my answer offends her deeply. "We've already eliminated C." She whacks her pointer to number seven on the board, and sure enough, there's the C with a slash through it.

Oops. How did I miss that? Was it on the board this whole time?

Mrs. Pak opens her mouth to continue when the timer suddenly goes off.

It's noon. *Phew!*

"Okay, class. Finish this problem set and do practice exam number four tonight for homework," Mrs. Pak says over the commotion of everyone packing up to go. "You're dismissed," she adds, even though everyone has already started to trickle out.

"That was close," I whisper to Ginny.

"I'll say. You almost got Pak-attacked."

Ginny props her glasses on her nose. The way she does it triggers a memory of something I saw on TV. "Hey, did you watch the SNL clip I sent you? The one sketch where the guy with the binoculars steals the lion?"

"No, my parents don't like it when I watch that show." Ginny shrugs.

"Mine don't either, but you have to see it. It's the most hilarious thing ever."

She wrinkles her nose. "To be honest, SNL isn't really my kind of humor."

"Are you joking?" If that's not funny to her, what is? I can only shake my head. I truly cannot understand this girl sometimes.

Suddenly, Ginny's eyes light up. "But that reminds me of this documentary I saw on Animal Planet."

Here we go again. I can feel it coming. Depressing animal rant happening in three, two, one . . .

"So, it was about these lions in the savannah of Botswana," she says, as she launches into yet another passionate speech on the dire state of the planet. "It's horrific. These farmers are *killing* them for preying on their livestock." She walks faster. "Can you believe that?"

I shake my head.

"Endangered lions, Yumi." Her eyes narrow. "Endangered!" She sighs loudly. "It's the saddest thing ever."

"Ginny, you aren't . . . *lion*." I nudge her with my elbow. "Get it? Lyin'? Lion?"

She clutches her binder close to her chest and cuts me a sideways glance. "This is no laughing matter, Yumi. These lions are losing their habitats and getting slaughtered, and you're over here making jokes?" She comes to a dead halt right there in the middle of the sidewalk. "Can you imagine what it's like trying to survive in an environment you aren't suited for?"

I kick a pebble down the cracked sidewalk. Sadly, I can.

That's just how it feels every day I'm at Winston. Talk about an unsuitable environment. It's basically a shy person's worst nightmare. I'll never know why the teachers there are so obsessed with group projects, presentations, debates, discussions, and, my personal favorite, icebreakers. I think I sweated more last year than all my other ten years combined. And then there's my loner status. It's supposed to be one of the most prestigious prep schools or whatever, but going there makes me want to hide in my shell like the tortoise I saw on the Animal Legal Defense Fund article Ginny gave me the other day.

She pushes the button for the crosswalk at the corner of Wilshire Boulevard and Western Avenue. "Want to come over to my house? The new BTS video just dropped."

There's a flutter in my chest at the mention of my favorite K-pop band. "Wish I could, but I have to go study at the library. Mrs. Pak has me on her 'intensive plan,'" I say with air quotes.

"Class plus three hours of independent study at the library?" Ginny nods knowingly.

"Yup." That's the one.

"Yikes, Mrs. Pak put my brother on that same plan

when he was studying for the SATs." She rolls her eyes. "It's like she knows there's bad Wi-Fi there."

"Right? It's a total connectivity black hole." I groan. It's not even worth trying to stream anything on their ancient computers. Trust me, I've tried. Thanks to Mrs. Pak's *intensive plan*, I'm struggling to keep up with Jasmine Jasper's vlog.

"Well, hang in there."

"Thanks, bye," I say as we go our separate ways.

I'm waiting for the light at the crosswalk when a bus comes roaring down the street farting a giant carbon monoxide cloud right at me like I'm not even there. I wave my arms to clear the air, but then the signal changes and a throng of earbud-wearing pedestrians, moms pushing strollers, and college students with backpacks rush at me with a vengeance. I dodge and sidestep my way across as fast as I can.

I'm almost at the library when something catches my eye.

There's a guy up on a ladder filling in the marquee on the side of the building that just went up.

Sweet, a movie theater!

I don't care what Dad says; I'm excited about the businesses coming into my neighborhood. The coolest stores on the block are the new ones. Like the cute boba café, the indie comic bookstore, and now a movie theater.

I scamper closer to see which movies will be playing.

To my utter shock, the marquee reads WELCOME TO THE HAHA CLUB.

It's not a movie theater—it's a comedy club!

I'm suddenly light-headed. How did this come to be? It's as if my subconscious wished it into existence. I've never actually seen a comedy club in real life, but now there's one right here. I have to check this out!

Ever so casually, I stroll past the door to steal a peek inside but immediately stop dead in my tracks at the life-sized poster of the one and only Jasmine Jasper hanging on the lobby wall. JASMINE JASPER AT THE HAHA CLUB AUGUST 3–14!

Holy Hot Cheetos, is she going to do some shows here? I've only ever seen her on YouTube, but of course she must perform at comedy clubs, too.

In the poster, she looks absolutely flawless holding a

microphone like the comic queen that she is. Everything about her commands attention: her bright red lipstick, her cute outfit, and of course her signature pixie haircut.

I must get a selfie with her poster. It'd make the ultimate profile picture.

After scoping out the premises, I sneak inside and take a quick snap of myself leaning back-to-back with her like we're best buddies. Since that's what we are in my mind. I pick my favorite filter, tag it with every hashtag I can think of, and post it.

I'm halfway out the door when the unmistakable sound of Jasmine Jasper's melodious voice comes on the PA system. "How is everyone doing today?" she whoops.

My heart skips a beat.

It's her. She's here. Like right here in this very building!

Shivers run down my spine. Jasmine Jasper and I are breathing the same air right now. I'll just take a glimpse. It'd be stupid not to.

Quietly, I tiptoe down the dark hall leading to the main auditorium and poke my head in the doorway like a total creepster.

I cannot believe my eyes.

CHAPTER 5

There she is. Standing onstage right there across the room from me. How is this my life? She looks effortlessly chic in her flowy paisley-print skirt and sleek sleeveless top. Her dark brown skin glows under the bright lights. The rose-gold bangles on her arm clink together as she flips through some papers on a clipboard.

Finally, she speaks in her booming voice. "Who's ready for day two of summer camp?" she hollers. "Because we're about to get an ab workout with all the laughing we're about to do."

Ah, she's not here to perform. She's here to teach comedy camp!

The kids seated in the front of the darkened room clap and cheer.

Wow. It's hard to believe that I'm inside an actual comedy club. I don't know how many times I've looked up famous venues just to imagine myself in them: The Groundlings, Laugh Factory, The Comedy Store, The Second City. And now here I am, standing in the back of one. I marvel at the room for a second and take in the simple stage, curtains, and rows of chairs. This is where the magic happens.

I'm so caught up in the moment that I almost miss it when Jasmine Jasper abruptly stops to peer through the bright lights. "Is there someone back there?" She squints, cupping her forehead with one hand.

Uh-oh. She stares right at me.

"I see you hiding in the back." Her voice rings from across the auditorium.

Me? I point to myself.

She nods. "Yeah, you."

I need to get out of here! I pivot to make a quick exit, but my shoe catches on my laces, taking me down to the ground with a giant thud.

She winces. "That had to hurt."

I scramble to my feet. "I'm fine—I was just, uh—"

"Come here." She waves me over.

When I don't come closer, she laughs. "Don't be scared, my breath isn't *that* bad."

I do as I'm told and make my way down the stairs toward her. I'm both mesmerized and confused. I've lost control of my body and mind.

"You 'kay?" she asks kindly, flipping again through her clipboard.

"Um, yes, thank you." I mean, I'm not. My knee is throbbing, and I'm about to pass out from shock. But I've also met my hero, and I can now die happy and fulfilled. #blessed.

She scribbles something down. "You been on vacay, Kay Nakamura?"

"Huh?" Kay Nakamura? Is that some kind of fancy vacation destination or something?

"I'm messing with you." She flashes her dimples. "We missed you yesterday, but I'm glad you're finally here." She curls her finger. "Come on, now, you've got some catching up to do."

My heart stops. I realize what's happening. She thinks I'm a camper named Kay Nakamura.

This is very bad.

She shouts, "All right, let's get started." Another cheer rises from the fellow campers.

"Wait. No," I whisper.

"Take a seat, Kay." Jasmine points to where the rest of the campers are sitting.

Before I can explain, she bellows, "Okay, now I need some volunteers." A bunch of hands shoot into the air.

"But. But . . . Uh. Excuse me," I say, sitting down, but no one can hear me above all the kids shouting, "Me! Me!" "Pick me!" "I haven't gone yet" and "Ooh, oooh, oooh!"

I glance toward the exit. I'll only draw more attention to myself if I try to leave now. I suppose it couldn't hurt to stay and watch for a few minutes. I take off my backpack and set it down by my feet.

Jasmine Jasper selects a pudgy kid with some serious sideburns. He does a full-body fist pump and dashes onstage.

"Our first warm-up is called the World's Worst," Jasmine explains. "Remember, this is improv. That means you have to make it up as you go. There is no script. If you get stuck, take a breath and keep going."

Eeeeesh. Making up something funny? Without any practice? Right there on the spot? I sure am glad I'm not that guy.

"When we're doing these exercises, let's focus on listening, commitment, and stage presence. These drills are a great way to build skills that'll help you later in your stand-up."

They're going to do stand-up, too? That's so cool.

"For this round," she continues, "you're going to act out your idea of the worst zookeeper ever. You ready, Felipe?"

He thumps the giant *S* on his Superman T-shirt. "Super ready."

"That's what I like to see." Jasmine chuckles. "Go!"

He squeezes his eyes shut and buries his face into his elbow. "AAAAaaaa AAAAAaaaa AAAACHOO." He opens his mouth to speak, but then holds up one hand like he's about to sneeze again. "Excuse me." Another false start later, he finally says, "I don't know if I'm cut out for this. Feathers, fur, scales are my kryptonite." He clears his throat. "Allergies."

I giggle to myself. This Felipe guy's deadpan humor is on point.

Jasmine calls up the next kid, a freckle-faced girl wearing a furry orange vest. She tosses her head, sending her giant halo of frizzy brown hair flying in every direction. "Mates, don't waste your life being caged up!" she yells in an Australian accent as she pretends to unlock a door. "Live your best life and be freeeeeeeeeeeeee!"

Her arms flail as she stretches out her last word.

"That's a pretty convincing Aussie accent, Sienna," Jasmine says.

"Thanks, I've been working on it in drama class."

Next, Jasmine looks over at me. "Let's have our new friend, Kay, take a turn."

I freeze. My body and brain have disconnected, and I'm on standby status.

Loading. Loading. Loading.

"Come on, now. Everyone's waiting for you." Jasmine bobs her chin at me and motions to the stage.

"N-no, no. I can't." My words trip over themselves on

their way out of my mouth. "I—I'm not supposed to be here. This isn't for me. I'm not—"

"Hey, hey. Calm down." Jasmine puts her warm hand on my back. "We've all been there. It's hard to get onstage and perform, especially on your first day of camp."

Then she claps her hands three times, and the kids clap the same rhythm back to her.

What the . . .

Jasmine strides past us in her red suede fringe boots. She raises her palms. "Can we give our friend Kay some encouragement?"

And like a cult, they all chant in unison. "You can do it." Clap. "You can do it." Clap-clap. "We believe in you, Kay."

That was totally weird.

I am a stranger in a strange land.

Now what am I supposed to do? I go over the options in my head. I sure as heck don't want to go up there, but I don't want to let Jasmine Jasper down either. Everyone is staring at me. I have to do *something*.

A round of applause erupts as I approach the stage.

The heat from the spotlight beats down on my shoulders. I wipe my sweaty hands on the sides of my jeans. I keep my eyes focused on the blank wall right above everyone's heads.

It's then that I realize that these people don't know me. They think I'm a girl named Kay Nakamura. What do I have to lose? I'm never going to see them again. Isn't this what Jasmine Jasper meant when she said "we have to fake it till we make it"? My tension releases like a popped zit.

I take a deep breath and go for it. I scrunch my face with my hands on my hips. "I'm never playing Uno with you sniveling beasts ever again." I give my nastiest side-eye. "Bunch of lion cheetahs."

And they laugh. They actually laugh!

The other two kids who went up, Felipe and Sienna, give me high fives. A rush of adrenaline floods my system.

"Kay, that was great. Aren't you glad you took a chance?" Jasmine Jasper says. My chest swells with a strange sensation I've never felt before. It takes me a second to realize what it is. The Comedian's High! Jasmine talked about this on her web series. She described it as "thick satisfaction that comes from making people laugh that coats your heart like maple syrup." I never thought I'd get the chance to experience this.

Wow. Being Kay sure is a lot more fun than being Yumi.

We do a few more rounds of improv before moving on to stand-up. Jasmine leads us in a bunch of zany activities to generate ideas for jokes. The entire afternoon flies by, and before I know it, it's time for dismissal. As soon as I'm in the lobby, reality hits me hard. Mom is coming to pick me up in front of the library in a few minutes. I have to hurry and get my butt back to the parking lot before my parents find out about my funny business.

I approach Jasmine to explain everything, but she's busy talking with some campers. I stand around for a while, waiting for a good opportunity to jump in to tell her, "Turns out I'm not signed up to be in this summer camp. I came in to take a look because I'm your biggest fan, and it kind of spiraled out of control. Big misunderstanding. I'm sorry for the trouble. By the way, my name is really Yumi Chung. Can you autograph my Super-Secret Comedy Notebook?"

No matter how many times I rehearse it in my head, it sounds way too random to say out loud.

Maybe I can leave and never come back. I look toward the door. It'd be easier than trying to explain everything. Would that be so wrong?

I lower my head and make a break for it.

I'm halfway out the door when someone calls, "Hey!"

I turn around.

It's Felipe, the kid with the sideburns. It's too late to pretend I didn't see him because we've already made eye contact. I wave politely and turn to leave, but then he starts jogging over in my direction.

"Kay, wait up!"

"H-hello," I say, my insides jiggly. Answering to that name makes me feel like I'm wearing someone else's retainers.

"Dude, I wanted to tell you, I really liked your zoo-keeper improv."

I break into a sweat. I'm not used to people striking up conversations with me. Last year at Winston, hardly anyone bothered to speak to me at all. My own history teacher didn't call on me for the entire first week of school because he thought I couldn't speak English. True story.

I feel that familiar cramp that forms in my side whenever I struggle with what to say next. I inhale deeply and channel Kay again.

"Your allergy thing was pretty funny, too." My voice comes out smooth and confident.

Felipe scratches his chin. "You think so?" He grimaces. "Was it okay? Not too over-the-top?"

His hesitation puts me at ease. I know exactly what he's feeling.

"No, are you kidding? It was hilarious!"

"You know what?" He twirls his wrist like he's trying to remember something. "Your zoo thing kind of reminded me of this clip I saw online. The SNL sketch where the guy carjacks the Jeep with the lions. Have you seen it?"

"Totally!" I'm so psyched he knows the sketch that a snort escapes from my nose, and I forget to be embarrassed.

"I love that show," we say at the exact same time.

Felipe curls his hands into binoculars over his eyes,

and instantly I know the part he's about to reenact.

"We're going on a safari. We're going on a safari," he sings, bobbing his head the way they did in the video. His impersonation is spot-on.

And, totally out of character for Yumi but not for Kay, I join him in his bobbing. "We're going on a safari," we sing together, before succumbing to a fit of giggles.

"SNL is the best." He extends his fist.

"One hundred percent." I bump his fist, beaming.

He checks the time on his phone. "Well, I gotta go, but I'm glad you finally showed up to camp. I'll see you tomorrow."

As I wave, my good mood fades.

It's too bad I'm not actually Kay Nakamura, so I could come back to comedy camp tomorrow.

Just then, my phone vibrates in my pocket.

The notification flag pops up on my lock screen. It's a text.

Mom: Almost there.

Oh shoot!

CHAPTER 6

I sprint the whole way across the parking lot to the Korea-town Branch Library. When I get there, it's exactly three o'clock. Mom should be here any minute. Breathless, I collapse onto the bench outside. What a crazy day!

Honk! Honk!

Our tan minivan pulls up, and I'm a bundle of nerves as I jump into the passenger seat.

Mom, decked out in a giant visor and driving gloves, takes my backpack. "How was studying?"

"The usual." I make it a point to look down so that she won't detect the lies hiding beneath my eyelids.

"Good."

Lucky for me, Mom is in a rare pensive mood and doesn't press for details. I manage to get through the short car ride to the restaurant by staring at the home screen of my phone, with Mom none the wiser.

The relief doesn't last long, however.

"Yumi, go help your sister," Dad barks as soon as I enter. "She's in the back."

Yuri's here again? The expression on his face tells me he is in no mood for answering questions. Dang, what's with my parents today?

I grab an apron and swing around to the dark and dank corner off to the side of the kitchen. Immediately I hear the lumbering sounds of the industrial dishwasher, which is not unlike a very small drive-thru car wash. It thrums and hisses as steam randomly escapes from the sides.

"Hey again," I call out to my sister, whose back is turned to me.

"Oh, thank God you're here!" Yuri shouts from behind a mountain range of dirty dishes, pots, and grills. "I'm drowning. Do you want to scrape or wash?"

Tough decision. It's like having to choose between using the porta-potty or going in the bushes. "Uh. Wash, I guess."

"Suit yourself." She steps aside so I can squeeze by the

trash can on wheels. I wash my hands in the double sink.

"So, why are you here again? And what's up with Mom and Dad? Why are they both so mad?"

"Let's just say it's been quite a day around here." She bangs a plate against the side of the trash can, sending bits of rice and banchan flying.

"Where are Tony and Joaquin?" They usually bus the tables and wash the dishes.

"They quit."

Oh shoot.

She hands me the scraped plate.

"Today?" I dunk it in the soapy water and place it upright in the pegged tray. "Just like that? No notice or anything?"

"Yup," Yuri says, clenching her teeth as she swipes the next dish with her rubber-gloved hand. "Mom and Dad called me in a panic a few hours ago, begging me to come in and help."

"They did?" A ripple of guilt runs through me. While I was giggling my butt off during improv warm-ups, my family has been in a state of crisis trying to keep this restaurant afloat.

My sister wipes the debris off another plate in one swift motion. "I mean, I'm happy to help and everything, but they've been calling me every other day with emergencies like this. It's like they don't understand that I have my own life now."

"That really sucks, Yuri." I spray the remaining sludge off the plates and send them down the conveyor belt into the dishwasher. "And you're so busy with the research you're doing in the lab, too."

She gets quiet. "Whatever. It's not a big deal. What's going on with you?"

A smile creeps over my face.

"What?" She puts down her plate. "Yumi Chung, tell me right now. What's the secret?"

"Don't tell Mom and Dad, but I had the most epic day of my life," I say in a lowered voice.

I load the next crate, yammering nonstop, filling her in on all the details of my wild afternoon as Kay Nakamura.

"You're so silly!" my sister says, laughing. She jiggles the trash can to make room for more waste. "Why didn't you tell them that you weren't Kay right away?"

"You know how I get sometimes. I just froze." I squirt some more detergent into the bucket of silverware.

"Only my little sister could accidentally steal someone's identity." She shakes her head with what looks like half amusement and half horror. "And I thought this sort of thing only happens in the movies."

"Right?" I gush. "That's exactly how it felt, like I was an actor playing someone in a role." I get the chills remembering the feeling of being in control, of being heard and maybe even appreciated. "It's weird, but I actually sort of liked it. A lot. It's as if I've discovered what I was born to do."

"That's phenomenal. People go their whole lives searching for that."

A faraway look passes over my sister's face. "Listen, I think you should seriously pursue this." Her wild eyes pierce into me with conviction.

"What are you talking about?" Who is this person,

and what has she done with my goody-two-shoes sister?

"I've been thinking about this lately, and we all need to follow our passions."

Passions? Who's talking about passions? Maybe Mom was right. Yuri does have a boyfriend.

She talks fast, and her rubber-gloved hands are moving even faster.

"Like, we can't live for our parents for the rest of our lives. At some point, we need to do what makes *us* happy!" She smacks the top of the trash can for emphasis.

It's like she's talking to me, but she's not.

"Oooookay . . ." I tilt my head. "What are you suggesting?"

"You need to ask Mom and Dad to sign you up for comedy camp."

I burst into laughter, nearly dropping my sink hose. My sister has lost it. Completely.

"No way."

I mean, yes, of course I wish I could go to comedy camp, but has she forgotten who we're talking about?

The same unnecessarily strict parental units that forbid us from painting our nails, borrowing friends' clothes, and going to sleepovers?

"I'm serious. Yumi, if you never stand up for yourself and go along blindly with whatever Mom and Dad say, you'll be chasing their dreams, not your own."

Dang, that's intense.

She slides off her rubber glove and touches my shoulder gently. "You should do comedy. Really. You owe it to yourself. Mom and Dad will support you eventually."

"I'm not so sure about that."

"Trust me. You just have to put an educational spin on it. I'll talk to them for you."

I shrug. What's the point? I already know what they're going to say.

Manuel comes in with another cart full of dirty dishes. "Ey, if it isn't the Chung sisters working the dish pit!"

I give him a soapy-handed high five. "Yuri just told me the bad news about Tony and Joaquin."

"Yeah, I'm gonna miss those guys." Manuel unloads the bussing buckets onto the counter.

"What the heck, though? They couldn't give us a little more notice? We're down to four part-time employees now. Did they have to leave us in the ditch like that?"

Yuri knots up the bulging trash bag. "I'm sure they had their reasons."

"She's right. Can't really blame them, cipota." He lifts the bag and flings it over his shoulder like Santa Claus. "Mr. Shin from the new gastropub down the street offered them a pay raise if they started right away. They gotta feed their families, too."

"Did he really?" Yuri asks.

"Did he offer you a job, too?"

"He did, but he couldn't offer me flexible hours for Sofia."

I breathe a sigh of relief. Mom lets Manuel set his own schedule because she knows no one can cook as well as he can.

"But if I left, you know I'd always be your uncle Manuel, right?" He flexes his biceps.

I giggle, flexing my muscles, too.

"C'mon, Yuri! Don't be too cool for us!" Manuel prods.

Yuri reluctantly holds up her arm and gives it a half-hearted pump.

"Atta girls!" He's halfway out of the room when he pokes his head back in. "Yuri, did you tell your parents about your . . . uh . . . thing?"

Her mouth curves into a shy smile. "No, not yet."

Um. What thing?

His eyes squint with disapproval.

Yuri sighs, and all the energy goes out of her body with it. "I don't know if they're going to understand . . ."

Oooh. This must be about her secret boyfriend!

"Can't keep them in the dark forever," he says before he leaves.

Why doesn't she want to tell Mom and Dad about this guy? Is he some kind of bad boy who cusses a lot? Does he have long hair, tattoo sleeves, and ride a Harley like the bad boys on TV? I need to know.

As soon as Manuel is out of earshot, I ask suggestively, "What was that about?"

She loudly shakes open a new bag and secures it around the lip of the trash can. "Nothing. I'll tell you later."

"Fine, then."

So she gets to ask me about my secrets, but she doesn't tell me anything about hers? I mean, honestly, she told Manuel about her boyfriend before me?

I guess I'll always be a baby to her.

We finish the rest of the dishes in silence.

A while later, Mom hollers at us, "Come eat!"

My stomach grumbles on cue.

Having grown up in a restaurant, I automatically get hungry at four o'clock on the dot, when the lunch shift leaves and we close the restaurant for an hour between meals. This is when we eat dinner.

My sister and I take our seats around the folding table in the office.

"Where's Manuel?" Mom asks.

"He couldn't make it today," I say. "He had to go pick up his granddaughter from day care."

"Aigoo, he should have told me so I can pack some for Sofia. She loves my bulgogi fried rice." Mom is a total sucker for chubby toddlers who eat well.

She fluffs the rice with a wooden spoon. "Eat a lot," she says, handing me a heaping plate.

As if she even had to tell me. I could honestly eat my weight in fried rice. Mom's got the gift of knowing exactly what'll hit the spot. I swear, she has a sixth sense about it. Her personal touch and hospitality were what made our restaurant the place to be. Back in its heyday, Park Chang Ro, the Korean pitcher from the Dodgers, even rented out our place for his wedding banquet. But as the new restaurants got sleeker and trendier around us, our cavernous place, packed to the gills with traditional Korean knick-knacks, got left behind. The food's still on point, though.

Yuri takes the bowl from her. "Here, Mom. You sit down and relax. I'll do this."

Mom nods and takes a load off.

"How was dishwashing?" She pounds her knee, massaging out the weariness.

"Well, it took us a bajillion times longer than it takes Tony and Joaquin, but we finished it." I shovel the rice down, savoring the crispy bits toasted by the bottom of the bowl.

"Hopefully we can find new dishwashers soon," Mom says, the worry lines creasing her face.

"I can put up a job posting on the UCLA classifieds," Yuri suggests.

"Ah, yes. Good idea." Mom's face brightens suddenly. "Speaking of the UCLA, how is your research job going?"

My sister pushes her dinner around with a spoon. "Same," she replies, without looking up.

Mom leans in. "There must be many Korean students in your laboratory. Are there any smart young men . . . ?"

Wow, subtlety is definitely not her strong suit.

"I have no idea." Yuri coughs once into her fist, and her eyes dart over to me. "Mom, did Yumi tell you about what happened today?"

I nearly choke on my fried rice.

"Why? What happened?" Mom's face contorts with concern.

I wipe my mouth with a napkin. "It's nothing."

"No, it's important to you. You should tell her," Yuri urges.

I glare at her, bristling. Is she really going to throw me under the bus? Just because she doesn't want to tell us about her love affair with Bad Boy, she has to tell Mom *my* secret? And for what? She knows more than anyone that our parents aren't the freewheeling types who spend big bucks to send their kids to fun places like Disneyland or comedy camp. Mom's idea of recreation is washing the dishes with the TV on. How am I supposed to explain something like the Haha Club to them?

"I—I . . ." The words jam in my throat like traffic on the 101 freeway during rush hour.

"I know." Mom's voice rises, full of hope. "You got the one hundred percent on your practice test today?"

"No, it's not that," I say, irritated that was her first guess. I scrunch the napkin into a tight little ball. "So there's this cool new place near the library." I gulp. "It's a . . . comedy club."

"Go on, Yumi." Yuri lowers her chin, coaxing me to continue.

"And it turns out they have this summer camp thingy there."

I look to my sister for help.

"Seems fun. Maybe you could sign me up?" I squeak.

The door swings open, and Dad trudges into the office.

"Sign up for what?" He plops down at the desk and clicks around on the mouse.

"This summer camp. Where I can learn how to tell jokes and stuff," I try to explain.

"Only in America they have this kind of nonsense." He scoffs. "Pay money to tell jokes."

Yuri steps in.

"I think it would be great for Yumi to attend a performing arts camp." She leans toward Mom and says in a lowered voice, "You know, so she can work on her . . . *communication skills.*"

Um, hello. I can still hear you. I'm right here.

"The camp has all these activities to help kids with their confidence. They practice speaking in front of groups. With Yumi being so shy and everything, this might be beneficial for her. She'll need these skills for college interviews, job interviews . . ."

Mom's brows bunch together the way they do when she's perplexed. My heart flutters. She's actually considering it.

But then Yuri goes all in and starts laying it on infomercial-thick. Her voice is eager. Too eager.

"I just checked out the website a few minutes ago. It looks like a worthwhile educational investment. For it being two weeks long, from twelve thirty to three, which is after hagwon, by the way . . . two hundred dollars is not a bad deal—"

Dad cuts her off right there. "Absolutely not," he barks. There is no question in his voice.

Yuri stops talking immediately.

I blink hard. His rejection feels like a giant anvil strapped around my ankle, yanking me off the cliff like in those vintage Road Runner cartoons. This is exactly why I never ask for anything. The disappointment hurts too much.

Dad gives Mom a little head bob. Mom's lips press into a line.

"Yumi, you have your exam coming up in a week and a half." She clears the plates from the table. "You do not have time to do any camp right now."

"You need to focus on getting the scholarship," Dad grunts from behind the monitor. "Anyway, we cannot afford to send you to camp right now. Hagwon is already expensive enough." He gets up from the desk. "You can read the joke book at the library for free."

"See?" I whisper to Yuri from across the table. "Told you."

I knew going in that my parents wouldn't understand why I'd want to do this, but why do I feel so disappointed?

Then, to make matters worse, Mom adds, "Also, Mrs. Pak called earlier. She wants to meet with you before hagwon."

Just great. What now?

CHAPTER 7

When I get to Mrs. Pak's office the next day, it takes three attempts to muster the courage to knock on the door.

"Come in," her voice blares from inside. How can such a small human have such a big voice?

The first thing I notice is the bulletin board full of pictures of high school students in graduation gowns behind her desk. Each portrait is labeled with the kid's name, graduation year, and university. Harvard, Princeton, Yale, Stanford, UC Berkeley, UCLA. I stifle a giggle when I spot Yuri's photo up there. She looks so babyish in her goofy Coke-bottle glasses and oversized cap and gown. And then I remember it's because she was barely fifteen.

Mrs. Pak, her back ramrod straight in her chair, catches me gawking. "You can be on my Wall of Excellence, too,

Yumi," she says, "if you learn to apply yourself." She folds her slender hands together under her chin. "Sit down." She gestures to the chair next to me.

I trip over my feet and stumble into the seat.

"I called you in here today because I want to discuss your progress."

She pauses.

"You aren't progressing enough," she says bluntly.

I flinch, but I'm not that surprised. Korean adults are all about talking without a filter. I can't count how many times I've been told "You need to pinch your nose so it's not so flat" or "Your sister is a genius. What happened to you?" My American side is offended, but my Korean side knows it's not a big deal.

"You haven't shown any significant growth since your diagnostic exam."

MRS. PAK'S HAGWON

REACHING FOR IVY LEAGUE DREAMS

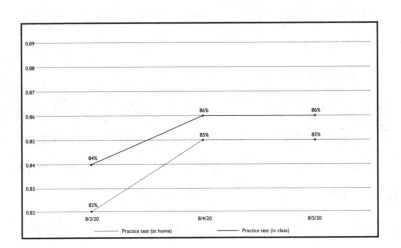

"Oh no." You could eat dinner on that thing. I'll have to jump more than ten percentage points in ten days in order to secure the scholarship.

"Don't despair." Mrs. Pak puts on her bifocal half-glasses, the kind that sit low on her nose. "The good news is you're a smart girl. Not a genius like your sister, but you know the material."

She pulls out a thick file folder from her cabinet and rustles through it. "However, you have to make some significant changes. Up here." She thumps her temple, then hands me a packet of my work.

"What do you notice about your tests?" Mrs. Pak watches me as I flip through the papers.

I don't see anything amiss, but I have to say something. "Uh, they're not bubbled in very neatly?"

"Ha! That's the least of your worries." She snatches the sheet from me. "Look here." She points to a geometry problem. "Your calculations are correct. You even bubbled in the correct answer initially." She points out the erase marks. "But then you second-guessed yourself and ultimately went with the wrong answer."

I tense up all over.

"You did that repeatedly."

She punches some numbers into a calculator with her long skinny finger. "If you had stuck with your original answers, you would have scored ninety-four percent, which is much closer to your goal."

Okay. Life returns to me. That's not so bad. Ninety-four percent is in the same neighborhood as ninety-eight percent, at least. I can handle that.

"You're letting this test get into your head. Why do you think that is?" She stares at me.

"S-sometimes I get a little nervous," I mumble.

Biggest understatement ever.

Mrs. Pak takes off her glasses. "Mm-hmm," she says, like she's mulling something over in her head.

It's silent for a moment. Then our conversation takes a strange turn.

"Yumi, what exactly are you afraid of?" She presses her hands on the desk like she's flattening the surface with her sheer force of will.

Uh. Is this a trick question? I mean, I know the answer, but I'm not about to say it out loud. I grip the sides of the metal folding chair and wait her out in silence.

But then she leans a little closer. "Yumi, what are you afraid of? Answer honestly."

I pick at my cuticles. "I guess . . . maybe I'm afraid . . . of you," I answer in a whisper.

Mrs. Pak puts one hand on her hip like she's going to level with me. "Think about it. I weigh one hundred pounds. Not nearly enough for an actual Pak Attack," she says with a trace of humor. "And we both know any grade I give you doesn't count for anything."

She taps the desktop with her perfectly manicured fingernail. "Ask yourself, why are you afraid of me?"

"I don't know." My voice cracks a little. "I guess I'm afraid to disappoint you and my parents and everyone else. I'm not as smart as my sister, so—"

"Wrong!" Mrs. Pak shouts. "Your problem is not your intelligence. Your problem is that you're hampered by your own indecision. Don't you see? Your fear of disappointment is holding you back. Like handcuffs. You need to stop worrying about failure and trust in your own instincts."

"But I don't know how."

"Well, Yumi, sometimes you have to pretend you're

more confident than you are until you become that way."

A chill runs down my spine, like someone threw a glass of ice-cold water at my face. Fake it till you make it. Just like when I was pretending to be Kay at the Haha Club.

Then Mrs. Pak scrawls something on a yellow legal pad. She tears off the sheet and presses it into my palm.

In neat loopy script it reads, *The only failure is not trying.*

"What's this?" I ask, grappling with what it means.

"This is your new motto. Stop worrying about living up to other people's expectations and pursue excellence on your own terms."

"Um. Thank you." I don't know what to do with it, so I fold it into quarters and put it in my pocket.

And before the moment gets too touchy-feely, Mrs. Pak adds, "I want you to copy this sentence one hundred times."

Like, by hand? Is she serious? How is *that* going to help me?

Mrs. Pak gets up from behind her desk and opens the door for me to exit. "It's due tomorrow."

CHAPTER 8

"Watch where you're going!" the mustached vendor yells right as I barrel into the colorful umbrella shading his elote cart.

"Sorry." I prop the umbrella upright and scurry past pedestrians down the street toward the library.

I'm so distracted, I can't think straight, let alone walk straight.

Even though it's been hours since meeting with Mrs. Pak, my brain is still swirling with questions. Could she be right about me? What would my life look like if I stopped worrying about what people think? I'd be able to order for myself at a restaurant and correct my PE teacher when she pronounces my name "Yummy." And maybe I'd stand up to my parents and actually make a case for going to camp at the Haha Club.

Whoa.

I might have solved the secret of the universe, but something stops me cold. From the corner of my eye, I spy a small shadow trailing me from behind as I cross Western Avenue. Is someone following me? I zigzag my way through the crowded crosswalk, but the shadow is right on my tail. My heart hammers against my ribs as I get to the other side. I consider my options. I could make a run for it or duck inside the Parisian-style Korean bakery.

But no. I won't.

I'm sick of being worried all the time.

In one quick motion, I pivot and shout, "Back off!" assuming the fighting stance I learned in tae kwon do when I was little.

"AHHHHHHHH!"

I'm a mere moment away from gouging the creep in the eye sockets with my two stiff fingers when it registers in my brain who it is.

"Felipe!" I utter, relaxing my trembling hands. "Sorry, I thought you were a kidnapper or something." I wasn't expecting to ever see him again.

Color comes back into his face. "Kay, I didn't know you did martial arts."

"I took tae kwon do for a few years, you know . . . just for kicks." I kick my foot up for flair. It feels like something Kay would do.

"Funny," he says with a chuckle. "Sorry about startling you. I wanted to make sure it was you before I said hi."

"Pshh. I wasn't scared." I shrug teasingly. "You're the one who screamed like a banshee."

"Excuse you. That was my supersonic scream." He takes a superhero stance with his chest puffed out and fists on hips. In a deep voice, he says, "I can shatter objects, level skyscrapers, and incapacitate my enemies using the power of my supersonic scream." Then he squeezes his eyes shut and screeches at the top of his lungs. "AHHHHH!"

I burst into laughter. "Felipe, stop! You're going to freak people out." I cover his mouth with my hand.

"Never underestimate the power of my scream, Kay." Then he does it again, punching his arms and doing kicks into the air. He yells, "KAPOW! BOOM! SMASH!" without a care in the world that everyone on the street is staring at him.

I love it.

We walk through the palm tree–lined boulevard past strip malls marked with signs written in Hangul, reenacting our favorite comedy sketches until we arrive at the Haha Club.

Felipe holds the door open for me.

I knew it was coming, and now here we are.

My moment of truth.

Do I go back to comedy camp as Kay or not?

I still don't know.

"Hey, I'm going to use the bathroom," I tell him, knowing full well I might not return.

"Sounds good. I'll see you inside." Felipe disappears through the hallway.

After closing the bathroom door, I splash water on my face.

What should I do?

Standing in front of the mirror, I search for answers, but only dark doubts crawl into my ear.

Look at yourself, Yumi. You aren't a comedian. You're an awkward, lanky Korean girl from Koreatown. You can hardly get through a conversation without a stomachache. You think you can make people laugh?

Onstage? You're not even that funny. And what are you going to do when the real Kay shows up? How are you going to explain that? What are Mom and Dad going to think when they find out? Is this really worth it?

I yank a paper towel from the dispenser and bury my face in it.

This is all too big to overcome.

A lump forms in my throat.

Maybe that's my answer: I can't. I ball up the paper towel and toss it toward the trash, missing by a few inches. Of course. When I reach to pick up the ball, something slips out of my pocket. It's Mrs. Pak's note. I unfold the sheet of yellow paper and read the words again.

The only failure is not trying.

Goose bumps prickle my skin.

Yuri's words haunt me, too. *If you go along blindly with whatever Mom and Dad say, you'll be chasing their dreams, not your own.*

Winston, hagwon, the SSAT. All that stuff is for my parents.

My jokes, those are for me.

That spark when I craft the perfect punch line, the satisfaction of coming up with a fresh take for a bit, the excitement of nailing just the right wording . . . it's the best. It makes me feel like what I have to say is worth listening to.

I inhale deeply as I stare intently at the mirror again.

Look at yourself. You made the whole camp laugh yesterday. You did that. Here at camp, you are funny and confident and you fit in. As Kay Nakamura, you have nothing to be afraid of. This is just the thing you were hoping for: a fresh new start.

I pick up the paper-towel ball from the ground.

This time I crouch, aim, and shoot. It lands in the wastebasket with a swoosh.

Score.

CHAPTER 9

By the time I get to the auditorium, it's too late to join Felipe in the front row, so I slide into an empty seat in the back. I guess I'm really doing this.

My heart races as Jasmine Jasper goes over announcements onstage. "We've got a bit of a rodent problem in the building, so please no food or drinks in the auditorium. I'm not about that hide-and-squeak life."

She wiggles her fingers and puckers her face with her tongue hanging out like she's had some sour kimchi.

I giggle. Yeah, this is where I'm supposed to be.

Jasmine continues. "This Saturday, I'll be hosting a community service field trip to the nursing home around the corner. It can get kind of lonely there for some folks, so I thought it'd be fun to do a little show for them. Tell some jokes to lift their spirits. If you're interested in joining me, meet me here at ten and we'll walk over together. Totally optional, but it'll be fun!"

I jot down the date.

"And lastly, mark your calendars. Next Thursday, we'll be performing a special stand-up showcase here at the Haha Club. It's going to be poppin', so get the word out to your friends and family now."

Friends and family? The thought of my parents watching me tell jokes onstage makes me twitch. Maybe coming back here was a mistake. If Mom and Dad ever find out what I'm up to, they might just grill me. On the barbecue.

I'm contemplating hightailing it out of there when Jasmine does her three-clap thing and, like I'm in a trance, I clap back the rhythm with the other campers, shaking off my hefty thoughts.

Logic returns to me. Mrs. Pak said that I have to stop living my life in fear and start pursuing excellence on my own terms. Sure, she wasn't talking about this camp exactly, but it certainly applies here, too. What better place is there to learn how to get people to listen than a comedy club?

My stomach settles as I sit back in my seat.

"For our warm-up today, we're going to talk about the 'Yes, and' principle of improvisational comedy," Jasmine explains. "It's basically the idea that you should accept what the other person has stated with a *yes*, then expand on that line of thinking with an *and*.

"That means you have to go with whatever your groupmates come up with, no matter how bonkers it is. This practice of layering will help your joke composition for your stand-up. Make sure to pay attention to your partners' body language and tone, because the goal is to tell a story together."

She raises three fingers. "Before we start, I need everyone to get into groups of three."

Instead, I break into a sweat. Everyone scrambles into groups, but I hesitate, standing there like a giant dork. I get flashbacks of being in biology lab at Winston all over again. Alone. Pathetic. Without a group to call my own. Needing the teacher to assign me to one.

But then, from the other side of the room, Felipe hollers, "Kay! Join us." He's with Sienna, who is sporting an oversized black beret today.

"Yeah, c'mon, Kay," she says, beckoning me with both arms.

That's right. I stand up tall. Here at the Haha Club, I'm Kay, and Kay has no problems making friends.

Jasmine explains, "The premise of the sketch is you're on a family road trip. Each person will act out a given emotion. For the first set, the emotions are"—she reads from her clipboard—"angry, hungry, and scared."

She looks up expectantly. "Now, who wants to start?"

Sure as heck not me. I look down at my shoelaces to avoid eye contact. There's no way I'm going up there without watching a few groups go first.

But then Sienna starts flailing her arm in the air like she urgently needs to use the bathroom.

"Oh, someone came with her game face on. And game . . . hat." Jasmine smiles broadly.

"Thanks, it's my dad's," Sienna replies.

I take another look. What kind of dad wears a beret like that? Is he a French painter? Or a mime? This girl is so intriguing.

"Okay," Jasmine says, "I'll give you a minute to decide your roles."

Sienna wants to do angry, Felipe takes hungry, and I'm left with scared. Which is appropriate, because that's precisely what I am.

Too soon, Jasmine cues, "Action!"

Felipe starts us off. He taps Sienna on the shoulder. "Mom, are we there yet?" he whines, resting his chin on his fist.

Sienna's face scrunches, and magically she transforms into a Texan mom with a serious mean streak. She roars, "Yes, and I told you a million times! Quit your bellyaching." She grabs ahold of her hat like a steering wheel. "Or I'll throw your complaining little heinie out the window!"

A tittering of laughter comes from the audience.

Then Felipe grabs his midsection and moans from the chair behind her. "But, Mooooom, we've been driving for eighty-two hours straight. I'm so hungry, I'm going to faint." He drapes his hand over his forehead and wobbles a bit before his body goes limp, sliding to the ground in a puddle.

A few people laugh.

Is he done? My chest pounds like there's a wood-pecker in there. Should I go now? Is it my turn?

Felipe and Sienna are looking at me. Yes. It's definitely my turn.

Just like yesterday, I try to access my inner Kay, but for some reason it isn't working. I can't think of anything! This is not how it's supposed to go. I feel like puking.

If I don't say something now, I'm going to have a full-fledged panic attack in front of everyone.

Clasping my hands over my eyes, I come up with the most obvious unfunny thing ever.

"Yes, and, uh, I'm scared," I utter in a near whisper.

It's deathly quiet.

I peek between my fingers to see everyone staring back at me. Oh shoot, they're waiting for the punch line.

I knock my heels together in hopes, by some stroke of magic, that I'll be teleported home like Dorothy in *The Wizard of Oz*. But nope, I'm still here. And everyone is still waiting.

Finally, Jasmine Jasper claps, and the campers get

the hint and join her. "Okay, so remember this improv activity is all about creating a story together." She shoots us a strained look. "I gotta be honest. I didn't see that happening here."

Dang, I thought only my Korean aunties dropped truth bombs like that.

"She does not play around," Felipe mutters to us.

"Listen, you can't simply go down the line, each person saying one bit after another. That's not a story. Improv isn't about hogging the attention. It's about give and take. You've got to work together to find the humor *as a group*." Jasmine catches my eye. "Don't overthink it by trying to be clever. I want you to listen and react to each other. It'll be funnier if you let go and take a risk."

Has she been talking to Mrs. Pak or something?

Then she says the worst imaginable thing. "I want you to try it one more time."

I groan inside as we take our positions on the stage.

Before Jasmine Jasper can cue us, the campers break out into the Encouragement Chant. "You can do it." Clap. "You can do it." Clap-clap. "We believe in you."

This chant is corny, but oddly, it makes me smile. I take

a deep breath, and it flushes out my million worries. I inhale and focus on being laid-back and cool, like Kay.

The only failure is not trying.

The only failure is not trying.

Breathe. Breathe.

Sienna catches my eye and mouths, "You got this."

"Action!"

Felipe starts us off by tapping Sienna on the shoulder. "Are we going to exit anytime soon, because lunch was a while ago . . ." He rubs his tummy in circles. "I feel like if I don't eat soon, I'm going to turn—uh, to the dark side."

Sienna's eyes light up, and she pulls her beret down over her face and breathes heavily. "Luke, if you do not stop complaining, I will have no choice but to use the Force on you," she bellows like Darth Vader.

There's an eruption of surprised laughter.

Felipe scowls, feeding off of her energy. "I'm just so hungry! I'm so hungry I could eat a Wookiee right now."

Oooh, I've got something.

I crouch in my seat, my eyes darting wildly, and let out my very best Chewbacca roar.

"WAGRRRRWWGAHHHHWWWRRGGAWWWWWWRR!"

Then I clutch the red velvet curtain off to the side and hide under it like it's a blanket.

"Cut!" Jasmine Jasper shouts while applauding. "Now, that's much better. Good teamwork this time."

We walk offstage feeling ten feet tall.

During our snack break, Felipe, Sienna, and I are in the lobby doing a play-by-play recap of our sketch, reliving our performance like it happened twenty years ago.

"And then Kay grabs the curtain"—Felipe fights to get the words out between laughs—"and hides under it."

Sienna's slapping her thigh. "That was . . ." She wipes the corner of her eye with one finger. "Peak hilarity."

"So was your Darth Vader voice," I say. "I will have no choice but to use the Force on you." I mimic her in the deepest voice I can, which turns out not to be very deep at all.

"Kay, you sound like a whale," she says.

"I doooooooooo?" I say in my best whale vocalization. It feels good to make her laugh.

Sienna nudges me with her elbow. "Forget Star Wars, you should audition for the next Finding Nemo movie."

"Hey, speaking of auditions," Felipe says, taking out his vintage Avengers lunch tin. "My mom told me about PAMS."

"PAMS?" I ask. "That spray stuff in the can? The better butter substitute?"

"No, you goof." Sienna shines her apple on her tie-dye shirt. "It's this new junior high they're opening a few blocks from here. It stands for Performing Arts Magnet School."

"Performing Arts?"

"Yup, and get this." Felipe tilts his chin. "The school is going to have a comedy department. First of its kind in Los Angeles."

Hang on, what? "A comedy department at a junior high school? Is that a thing?"

"Yes, they're going to get *professional* comedians to teach guest workshops." Sienna bites into her apple.

"Cool, right?" Felipe spears his fork into a mango slice sprinkled with chili powder. "Sienna's mom told my mom all about the auditions at pickup yesterday. She said she's on the board for the school." He elbows her. "How come you never told me your parents are famous Hollywood big shots?"

She shrugs.

"They are? That's so cool! What do your parents do?" I ask.

She says quietly, "They're filmmakers."

Felipe is indignant. "Uh. Why are you selling them short? They're the masterminds behind the entire Dark Squad franchise!"

My jaw drops. *Dark Squad II* caused me to sleep with a night-light for a solid month.

"Your parents are so freaking cool."

While Sienna's parents made *Dark Squad I, II,* and *III,* my parents make lunch combos I, II, and III. Life is so unfair.

"So what's it like having them as your parents?" Felipe's eyes bulge with curiosity.

She picks at the stem of her apple. "I don't know. They're . . . unconventional."

"Is it true that they don't believe in homework and let you decide if you want to go to school or not?" Felipe asks. "They said that in an interview once."

"Kind of. They think school can kill creativity, but

I actually like homework and school." She clears her throat. "Anyway, back to PAMS. Are you going to audition?"

"I think so." Felipe nibbles on a mango slice.

Sienna nearly coughs up her apple. "Really?" she squeals. "Really, really?"

"Yup, my parents were totally into it. They can't stop talking about how I'm going to be a Mexican Conan," he says, busting out Conan's signature String Dance.

Sienna joins in on the dance. "I can't believe we might be going to the same school! This is the best news ever!"

Lucky.

Then Sienna turns to me. "Now *you* have to audition, too, Kay."

"Me?"

"Yes, you." Sienna slings her arms across our shoulders. "How fun would it be if the three of us went to PAMS *together*? All you have to do is fill out the registration, get some recommendations, and show up for the audition. August eighteenth."

If only I could.

"I don't know, guys," I say, with hesitation.

"Think about it. We can hang out every day and take classes together." Sienna gets more and more animated, her hair and hands flying in every direction. "It won't be the same without you."

My heart skips a beat. This is the first time in a long time I've felt like I actually belong in a friend group.

"You need to apply," Sienna says. "Doesn't it sound perfect?"

I pause.

It does.

Going to PAMS would be a dream come true. Hanging out with Felipe and Sienna every day, doing comedy, meeting real comics. Not setting foot in Winston's stuffy old halls again. What more could I ask for?

"Well, what's holding you back, then?"

Fear.

Felipe fishes his phone from his pocket. "Here, I'll text you the link to the website so you can check it out with your parents."

Parents. I sigh deeply.

How am I supposed to get Mom and Dad on board?

As we're exchanging numbers, the challenge looms heavy on my mind. It's going to be hard to convince my parents. Nearly impossible, even. But unlike before, I'm determined to make this work. I just have to.

month: AUGUST

8/8 Nursing Home field trip

8/13 ★ Camp SHOWCASE! ★

8/14 Last day of hagwon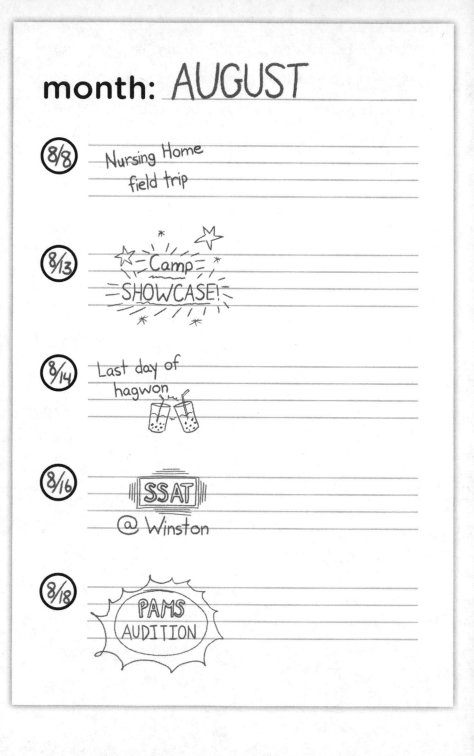

8/16 SSAT @ Winston

8/18 PAMS AUDITION

CHAPTER 10

Now that we've closed the restaurant and almost everyone else has gone home, Manuel and I take a break in the back office.

"Dinner service kicked our butts tonight." I hand him his favorite soda, Cuzcâtlan cola champagne, from the mini fridge. We didn't even have that many customers, but we were short-staffed again with the line cook out sick, so I had to fill in in the kitchen. While Mom and Dad took care of the front of the house, Manuel and I scrambled around, splitting our time cooking and cleaning. Needless to say, we got the slam.

"We survived, though. Didn't we?" Manuel gulps down his drink and wipes his mouth with the back of his hand.

I grab my Super-Secret Comedy Notebook from the desk. "This reminds me of a joke."

My superpower is invisibility. I'm still figuring out how to activate it. So far, the only time I can get it to work is when I'm around boys I like or when we pick teams for PE class.

He laughs. "You gotta keep this stuff for when you're big time and selling out the Staples Center." He tosses his empty bottle in the recycle bin. "You know, I sense something different about you . . ."

"About me?"

He rubs his chin and takes a long look at me. "You've been practicing, haven't you?"

Pangs of paranoia surge through me.

"Yes. I've been practicing, I mean. By myself at home. Yep. As one does," I say with a shaky laugh.

There's no way he could possibly know about my forays to the Haha Club, is there?

He punches out his time card and looks at me the way I look at myself in the mirror after a bad perm.

I hold my breath. If Manuel knows, he's totally going to tell Mom and Dad, and then I'll be doomed.

But to my relief, he smiles. "It's working. You've gotten better!"

Phew!

"Thanks for noticing." I release the air from my lungs. It's just my imagination on overdrive.

"Good job today in the kitchen." He grabs his jacket and keys from the hook on the wall. "I gotta go get Sofia. Vaya pues, kid."

It isn't until I hear the door shut behind him that I relax. I have until Mom and Dad finish closing up to work on my bit. I turn back to my notebook and start underlining the parts that made Manuel laugh. Which, it turns out, was most of it. Not bad, Yumi Chung! Maybe I can use this one for the showcase or even the PAMS audition.

If I can convince my parents to let me audition in the first place.

Overwhelmed, I throw my head backward and spin in circles in the office chair until the room is one continuous blur. And then there's that field trip to the nursing home coming up, too. How am I supposed to get them to say yes to any of this?

Everything is whirling, and I feel like I'm at the base of Mount Everest without a map. Or shoes.

I hear the door open and plant my foot on the ground to stop the chair.

The room is still spinning, but I make out my sister's slender silhouette.

"Hey, Yooms." She drops her purse on the empty chair.

I steady myself. "You're here *again*?" I'm glad to see my sister, but it's the third time this week she's come to the restaurant. "Are you sure you're still in med school?" I joke.

"Not funny." She shoots me a look of death and sits at the computer.

What's eating her? "So, why are you back here, anyway?"

"I came to talk to Mom and Dad." Yuri pulls up the day's point-of-service report from the accounting program and clicks through a few spreadsheets.

"About what?"

She points to the computer screen, ignoring my question. "These figures can't be correct. Are you telling me that this is all the money we made this week?"

"I guess."

"That's terrible. If you consider the variable costs and fixed costs—" She stops to do the calculations in her head. "Our break-even point in dollars is $5,720.30 for this month."

"So?" I hate it when she talks to me in genius and expects me to understand what the heck she's saying.

"That's abysmal." She closes the financial report. "Enough about that." She turns her attention back to me. "What's going on with you? Any luck convincing Mom and Dad to send you to comedy camp?"

Guilt crashes down on me like a tsunami. I never lie to my sister. "Uh." My mouth becomes dry. "N-nope. No luck there."

I change the subject. "Have you ever noticed how Mrs. Pak always touches her hair with one hand before she Pak-attacks? Like this?" I'm in the middle of doing a dead ringer Mrs. Pak impersonation when Dad comes in.

"Yuri, I thought I heard your voice."

"Dad. Yes, I came because I wanted to talk to you and Mom about something really—"

But Dad cuts her off.

"Yobo!" he shouts down the hall to Mom. "Our daughter is here."

A half second later, Mom pops her head in.

"Yuri, did you eat?" It's her multipurpose greeting. Kind of like "aloha." It can mean "hello," "goodbye," "I love you," "are you hungry?" or all of the above.

"I can heat up delicious kalguksu," she offers. "I made it with the clam."

No matter how beat Mom is after a grueling day at the restaurant, if she hears us utter the word *hungry*, the stove will be fired up in ten seconds flat.

Yuri shakes her head. "No, I'm fine."

Mom scowls, wiping her hands on her apron. "You

have to eat if you want to be a good student." She grabs my sister's twiggy arm and shakes it. "Lost too much weight. Cheeks are empty like a skeleton!"

I take a second glance at her. My sister's always been on the petite side, but my mom's right. She looks a little gaunt, and her collarbones are extra pointy through her silk tank top.

"I said I'm fine." Yuri tugs at the hem of her cardigan, hiding her body.

"The boyfriend doesn't like when girls are *too* skinny." Mom gives Yuri a knowing look.

I swear, this secret boyfriend has become Mom's favorite topic of conversation.

"What are you talking about?" Yuri says, incredulous.

I can't tell if my sister is playing dumb or if she's really clueless that we're onto her. We've *been* onto her.

Dad interrupts. "Everybody, come here. I have something to show you."

He shuttles us out to the main dining room and into one of the empty booths.

"Important family business," he says.

"What is it?" Mom leans over and pounds her own

shoulder with her fist, massaging the weariness from her back. After a fourteen-hour day on her feet, she doesn't look too keen on listening to one of Dad's little speeches.

Dad, however, is revved up and ready to go. "Listen, I have a plan to bring new business to our restaurant." He shakes out some blueprints from a cardboard poster tube onto the table.

This ought to be good. Dad's full of interesting ideas. Like the time he tried to solve our backyard rodent problem by hanging giant mobiles shaped like predatory birds he made out of Styrofoam. Only for them to be eaten by rats. Or the time I broke my arm and asked him to help me put my hair in a ponytail, and he secured it with a nylon cable zip tie that promptly slid right off. He's got lots of hacks that work in theory, but not so much in the execution.

Dad spreads out the blueprints with his hands. "Koreatown is changing so much. If we want to stay in business, we have to make restaurant welcome for waygookin."

"Waygookin" is Dad's choice word for non-Koreans. But the actual translation is "foreigner."

"All the popular new restaurants are the kind the waygookin like. With the young guys with the tattoo. Loud music." He scratches his chin. "Maybe we need something new, too. Something hot. Then I figured it out."

He jabs the blueprint with his pointer finger, which in his case is his middle finger. "Our restaurant is so big. Look at this! So much empty space. Too much waste!"

He circles the spot on the blueprint by the back wall. "So we will put in a karaoke stage here in the corner."

"A karaoke stage?" Yuri and I look at each other with clenched teeth. This is a whole new level of out there, even for Dad.

"Imagine it." He swipes his hand in the air in the shape of an arc. "Entertainment! Big stage! Microphone! Big TV with song words!" His eyes brim with hope as he looks over at the dark corner of the restaurant where dusty calligraphy scrolls and bamboo fans hang on the walls alongside stacked boxes of soy sauce and cooking oil. "No restaurant has this kind of entertainment in Koreatown."

"Dad, I know *you* love karaoke and all, but . . ." Yuri's voice trails off. "You think that'll work? Here? At our restaurant?"

Dad scoffs. "Yes, it's perfect. Everybody loves to sing. And get great meal at fair price at same time. Best combo!"

I pull the blueprint closer to me. "So you're converting that area into an event space?"

Makes sense. It's kind of off to the side, semiprivate. And the acoustics are great.

"I actually think some artsy types might be into this," I admit. Maybe his idea isn't so wild this time.

"Yes, Chung's Barbecue will not just be a place to eat." He takes a breath. "It will be a place to be a star."

"People could rent it for poetry slams, open mic-nights, private parties . . . maybe even stand-up comedy," I add, my excitement growing with Dad's.

"Yumi, please. This is adult talk." Mom chastises me as she reaches to point at the middle section of the restaurant. "Yobo, this is terrible idea. If you build stage, you have to take out all these tables. We have to fill the tables. Not take it out!"

"Humph," Dad says, not appreciating her naysaying.

Mom clucks her tongue. She isn't done. "And what about construction cost? Too expensive."

"Manuel's brother, Oscar, is a contractor. He said he will give us a good deal."

"We don't need a stage. We need to update decoration. Take out antique furniture, put in new tile, paint the walls. Feels so old in here. Needs makeover. So much cheaper than construction. We have too many expenses right now. Yumi's hagwon, Yuri's medical school—"

Then, out of nowhere, Yuri drops a bomb.

"Actually, that's why I came here. I need to talk to you about that."

She swallows hard.

"You don't have to pay for medical school anymore," she declares, sucking out all the air in the room. "I dropped out."

We all freeze.

She did *what?*

We are too stunned to speak. The only sound comes from the clock ticktocking from the wall.

Yuri Chung has never quit anything in her life. This is the girl who limped the last quarter mile of her cross-country meet on a sprained ankle because she wanted to finish what she started.

Finally, Dad breaks the silence. "What do you mean?" he asks slowly, like he's talking to someone who's holding a loaded gun.

"I've been trying to find the right time to tell you." My sister tugs at her cardigan. "I quit two weeks ago," she says, her voice hardly above a whisper.

My eyes dart between Mom and Dad.

"You quit the medical school?" Mom repeats, like Yuri has confessed to committing a crime. "Why?"

"Because I don't want to be a doctor."

Mom's voice gets louder. *"Want?* What do you mean, *want?* To be doctor is a great privilege!"

"Not for me. I hate it."

Yuri looks up at Mom, her eyes shining but unafraid.

"Maybe I've never wanted to be a doctor. I only went to med school to make you happy."

I can't believe my ears.

"How can you say that?" Dad demands. "This for you, your future. You worked so hard already. Why you give up now?"

"Dad, I tried to make it through my first year. I tried so hard to like it, but it never got better." She takes a breath. "I can't sleep or eat. I'm constantly stressed and anxious. I'm losing hair and weight. I'm sorry, but it's—it's just not for me." She wipes her eyes.

Mom plants one hand on the tabletop to steady herself.

"What're you saying? You failed your classes? You need more books?" Dad yells frantically. "We can buy you more books."

Yuri exhales long and slow. "No, no. It's not that. My grades are perfect. I'm—I'm not happy. I just don't want to be there. I hate the blood. The cadavers. The guts. The organs."

She rubs her temples in circles. "I don't belong there."

I get it. This is exactly how I feel about going to

Winston. Sometimes you just know when you don't belong.

"Maybe you're not happy now," Dad says, "but you will be happy later when you are the doctor. You must be patient. It will pay off later."

"Don't you see?" Yuri's face is splotchy and red. "It's everything. I can't take the pressure to make someone well. I can't handle the burden of someone's life or death. I know for certain this is not what I want to do for the rest of my life."

"What you going to do, then?" Dad takes a seat next to mine and folds his arms in front of him. "How you gonna pay your rent and your bills?"

She sniffs. "I've been working at Starbucks on campus."

Mom clutches her chest with one hand.

"You're working in coffee shop?" She looks like she might collapse.

"Yes, right now I am," she snaps. "Look, I don't know what I want to do with my life yet. I still need time to figure it out. I need to get out of Los Angeles for once. I need to travel and see the world. I need to make my own choices."

Dad opens his mouth to say something, but then presses his lips shut, breathing hard through his nose.

"That's why," Yuri starts, looking them in the eye, "I've decided to join the Peace Corps. I'm leaving for Nepal at the end of the month."

A collective gasp swells up from the three of us.

"What is Peace Corps?" Mom and Dad ask at the same time.

"It's a program that sends volunteers to promote social and economic development in other countries." Yuri pushes away from the table and stands up. "I'm going to South Asia to help rural farmers develop clean agricultural methods that promote soil conservation. I'll be there for two years."

She gathers her jacket from the chair and takes the keys out of her pocket.

"I have to go. I'll call you tomorrow."

She starts for the door but stops, her back still to us. "I'm sorry if you're disappointed, but I have to do this . . . for myself," she says before slamming the door on her way out.

What just happened?

CHAPTER 11

When Ginny asks me if I want to swing by Boba Love with her after hagwon, I cannot refuse. A frosty, sugary drink with soft, chewy tapioca balls is exactly what I need to get my mind off my family drama before camp.

It's been full-on crisis mode since Yuri broke her Peace Corps news yesterday. Stressful doesn't begin to describe it. My parents have been relentless trying to get her to reconsider. They've attempted every strategy in the book: reasoning with her, begging her, even scolding her like a little kid. But Yuri hasn't budged one bit. To make matters worse, after the last blowup, she stopped answering her phone altogether. Every call, even mine, goes straight to voicemail.

My sister did the same thing last year when she was stressed out about her MCAT exam. She locked herself in her room and wouldn't answer the phone or door for a solid week. I wish she didn't feel the need to block everyone out, especially me. It's not like I did anything to her.

Hopefully they'll figure things out soon. I really need my sister back in my life.

If ever there was a time for a boba break, it's now.

The moment I open the door to Boba Love, the sweet aroma of milk tea greets me like a warm hug. The soft-pastel-colored walls and the upbeat K-pop music video playing on the TV instantly boost my mood.

"I love this song. J-Hope is basically my idea of the perfect human," Ginny says, sliding next to me in line. "Look at his cheekbones."

"I know, right?" I bop my head to the beat of the catchy music. Personally, I'm more Team Jungkook, but there's no denying J-Hope's appeal.

"What flavor are you going to get?"

"Taro slush." I don't bother looking at the menu on the giant wall-mounted LCD screen. There is no other flavor for me.

"I'm getting the mango. It's dairy-free." Ginny sifts through her zebra-print backpack for her wallet. "You know, because I'm vegan now," she reminds me.

Ginny has been a born-again vegan since she read an article about the cruel truth of the egg and dairy industry a few weeks ago.

I giggle. "So, if two vegans get into an argument, do they still have beef?"

"Gosh, Yumi, your jokes are so corny," Ginny groans. "I'll tell you who I have beef with. My mom."

"Uh-oh. Again?"

"You know it. She refuses to take my veganism seriously. She claims I need to eat meat to grow taller. Fake news!" Ginny stabs her extra-wide straw through the plastic lid. "I can't even. Just because I'm the shortest one in my class, she thinks I should eat animals and animal products?" She rolls her eyes. "Um, hello. It's called genetics. I'm short because *she's* short."

She takes a long sip of her boba drink.

Ginny's parents are paranoid about her being small for her age. I remember her telling me how they had her drinking this expensive mystery tea from a Chinese medicine herbalist—until she found out it was made from ground deer antlers—to stimulate her growth plates or something like that. Understandably, it didn't go over well when Ginny discovered what the ingredients were. She's been squabbling with them about it nonstop ever since.

"My mom said if I bring up veganism one more time, I'm grounded."

"Oh shoot. So what happened?"

"Now I'm on screen restriction." She shakes the boba balls loose from her straw. "I can't believe I'm on her bad side for wanting to prevent suffering." She sighs loudly.

The door jingles, and I nearly choke on my boba.

It's Felipe.

I don't want him seeing me outside of the Haha Club. It's too risky. I turn around in my chair so my back is to him and try my best to blend into the wall, but my disappearing act doesn't work.

Felipe calls out, "Hello!" and comes toward our table.

I have no choice but to wave back. "Hi, Fel—"

His eyes jump to my side. "Ginny?" he says, interrupting me.

"Felipe?" Ginny seems caught off guard.

"How do you guys know each other?" we all say at the same time.

We laugh, but inside I'm filled with terror.

Felipe thinks I'm Kay, and Ginny knows I'm Yumi.

There is no easy way to explain this. I have to think fast.

"This is so random," I say in my best confident Kay voice. "Such a small world. Ginny and I go to the same tutoring center," I explain to Felipe. Then I turn to Ginny. "And Felipe and I go to . . . are in the same . . . extracurricular activity thing."

"No kidding? Felipe was in my class last year," Ginny says. "What activity are you doing together?"

"Kay and I are in the same—"

"Kay?" Ginny's forehead puckers like she heard white rhinos are no longer endangered. "Who's Kay?"

Ack. There it is. Shoot. Shoot. Shoot.

"Kay?" I chuckle nervously. I go with the first thing that pops into my head. "Oh, that? Kay is, uh . . . It's my English name."

I'm hot under my skin.

"You mean, like an alias? Like Clark Kent?" Felipe suggests.

"What the heck, Yumi? You never told me that you have an English name."

I suddenly feel out of breath. "Yeah. Sure do. I go by Kay sometimes . . ."

I clasp my hands together to stop fidgeting.

"Isn't it fascinating how there's multiple names for the same thing? Like boba tea is also known as bubble tea, tapioca tea. I've even heard it called pearl tea once. Like in Taiwan or something. Which, if you think about it, is odd, since boba balls are soft and chewy and pearls are so . . . not." I clench my teeth into a fake smile. "Isn't that ironic?"

Ginny and Felipe give me the same confused look.

"Um, okay." Ginny arches her eyebrow. "Wait, what activity did you say you guys were in together?"

So much for my attempt to divert the conversation. At this rate, Ginny's going to make me blow my cover in front of Felipe before my boba is done. I need to get out of here.

I slide my thumb around the edge of my drink, gently

popping off the lid. Then I let out the loudest sneeze of all time. I throw my whole body into it like I'm the Big Bad Wolf.

"AAAAAACHOOOOOOOOOOO!"

There's so much force that it sends a tidal wave of freezing purple slush and bouncy brown tapioca balls right onto the front of my shirt.

"AHHH!" I yelp. I'm not even acting. It's way colder and messier than I anticipated. "It's so cold! It's so cold!"

"Oh no!" Ginny shrieks, grabbing napkins by the handful from the dispenser on the table.

Felipe is too stunned to speak.

"No, no. I'm fine." I get up from my seat. "I'll go see if I can wash it out in the bathroom. Excuse me."

"Here, you can wear this." Ginny starts taking off her shirt. "I have a tank top on underneath."

Felipe's face burns bright red, and he suddenly becomes super interested with whatever is on his phone.

"No, I couldn't do that."

"Yumi, please." She nods so hard and so fast I'm afraid she's going to make herself dizzy. "I insist."

She shoves the shirt into my hand.

"Are you sure?"

"There's no way you can study at the library in that," she says, pointing to the giant purple splotch freezing my entire chest. "The librarian keeps the air-conditioning on full blast."

"Library?" Felipe asks, glancing at his watch. "But aren't you going—"

"Ahh!" I shout again. "Sorry, the slush is seeping into the shirt." I pull at my hem. "Brr. Yeah, that's cold. I should probably get changed before I get frostbite."

I point to the bathroom. "Ginny, can you help me?"

"Sure," she says, gathering her stuff and following me down the hall.

"I'll catch up with you later, then?" Felipe says.

"Okay!" I call behind me as I rush to the bathroom with Ginny, feeling equal parts relieved and ashamed.

Crisis averted . . . for now.

CHAPTER 12

Getting cleaned up in the boba shop bathroom takes longer than intended, and by the time I get to the Haha Club, camp has already started.

I find a seat in the back row, hoping that no one notices the shirt Ginny lent me, which has EAT FRUIT, NOT FRIENDS loudly silk-screened across the front in hot pink letters. Quietly I take out my notebook and pen and try to follow along with the lesson Jasmine's teaching.

"There is no one braver than a comedian, and that's the truth. Think about it. We share things about ourselves that other people try to keep secret. Sad things. Controversial things. Even embarrassing things. For us, that's just more material for the show."

Eeesh, not sure what I missed earlier, but what she's saying feels wrong on so many levels. Mom and Dad raised me to hide my flaws, not broadcast them. *Show your best face. What will others think? Excel and bring your family honor.* These are the things my parents have etched into my brain since I was in diapers.

"So why do you think comics share this kind of stuff?" she asks us. "Why do we just love to lay it all out there for everyone to see?"

No one volunteers to answer.

"Let me ask you something. What do you do when someone offers to tell you a secret?" She pauses, then leans to the side with her hand cupped over her ear. "We are all about it, aren't we? Because who can resist a juicy secret? No one."

I giggle. So true.

"See, comics know this and feed off of that nosiness because it's a surefire way to hook the audience." She clicks the remote control in her hands, and a paused video appears on the screen behind her.

"Let me show you what I mean."

I recognize it right away. It's blurry and pixelated, but you can make out a slightly younger Jasmine opening as the emcee of the Kids' Comedy Festival. It's from her website. I've seen it so many times, I can practically recite the whole thing by heart.

JASMINE

How many of you guys grew up poor?
(tugs on the microphone cord)
People in the crowd hoot in response.

JASMINE

I grew up poor, but the funny thing is, I had no idea. I just thought we were environmentalists.

That's the way my mom spun it to us. Reduce, reuse, recycle.

Taking too long in the shower: reduce. "You won't blame a drought on us," she'd say.

All done with that food container: reuse. Boom—instant Tupperware.

Got holes in your clothes: sew some patches on those jeans and recycle. Because landfills.

It made sense to me.

(walks casually from one end of the stage to the other and waits for the crowd's laughter to fade)

JASMINE

We'd even pretend to be survivalists at night. We'd set up a tent in the living room and play cards by candlelight, and just for an added challenge, we wouldn't use any electricity at all.

It wasn't until I started going over to friends' houses, where they didn't do any of this, that I figured it out: we weren't trying to protect the planet—we were just poor. Poor people are saving this world! My mom is the *true* Captain Planet.

Jasmine clicks the remote again, and the video cuts to black.

"Did you see that?" she asks us. "My story made you feel like I was letting you in on something real, right? Like we're good friends and I'm okay being vulnerable with you because I trust you."

Whoa.

"See, when you share something authentic about yourself, people connect to you. And chances are, you're not the only person who has felt the way you're feeling." She walks slowly across the stage. "When you open up, the audience will listen and laugh with you because you've gotten them to care."

Her words nestle deep into the hungry cracks of my heart.

"Y'all ready to give it a try for yourselves?" Jasmine gives directions for our activity. "I want you to brainstorm some things you can use for your own stand-up material. Protip: the more raw it is, the better it's going to work onstage. Start with the things you're afraid to say out loud."

I rummage through my hagwon index cards and test-prep books and take out my Super-Secret Comedy Notebook from my backpack. For the longest time, I thump the back of my pen on a blank page. I mean, obviously I have buttloads of cringey stories, but none that I'd be comfortable sharing in front of perfect strangers. What would my parents think? Dad would probably walk on the hot charcoals of his own barbecue grills before admitting to anyone that our family is anything less than perfect.

But Jasmine Jasper is telling me to get vulnerable, which means I need to get vulnerable. With fifty thousand subscribers who love her on YouTube, it's clear she knows what she's talking about. If I'm serious about wanting people to listen to me, I have to do this.

The only failure is not trying.

I grip my pen and power through, listing the first things that I think of without stopping.

1. At Winston, I eat lunch in the bathroom because I have no one to sit with.

2. My sister is way smarter and prettier than me and everyone knows it.

3. My parents have never told me that they're proud of me.

4. No one has ever had a crush on me.

5. I wish I really was Kay Nakamura.

I look over what I've written, and my eyes burn at the sight of my deepest, darkest secrets listed out on the page. It's official: I'm the biggest loser in Koreatown.

I blow my bangs out of my face.

There's no way I can work any of this into my act. It's way too pathetic.

I'm staring at my pitiful list, waiting for the minutes to tick by, when Jasmine's shadow falls over my page.

"How's it going?" she asks.

"Fine," I fib, keeping a stiff upper lip.

She sees right through my fake *fine*.

"It's hard to put yourself out there, isn't it?" She sits in the empty seat next to me. "Some stuff is so embarrassing that you'd rather forget it ever happened, right?"

"My stuff isn't even funny. No one wants to hear about someone having a tough time."

She pats my back. "What about a broke mom raising five kids by herself? That sounds pretty tough to me."

My cheeks redden. "I didn't mean—"

"Listen, you can find humor in just about any situation. That's why comedy can be so healing. You just have to describe things in a way that is totally different from—sometimes the opposite of—the way people expect you to describe it. And I know you can do that." Then she says something that outright makes me blush. "Because you're original, and that's the best kind of funny."

Eeep. Is she serious?

"Me? You, uh, really think so?"

"Absolutely. Just remember: you have a unique point of view. There is only one Kay Nakamura."

Uhhh. Well, two, technically.

"You have to believe in your story and your voice." She winks at me. "Once you've got that figured out, you're going to bring down the house. I can't wait to see what you come up with for the showcase. Your parents are going to be so proud of you."

Her words sink into me, filling me with brightness and hope.

For a moment, I dare to imagine how that'd go. I picture Mom and Dad sitting in the front row, watching from a full house. I'd tell some killer jokes, and they'd be so funny my parents wouldn't be able to hold it in. Mom would try to be demure by holding her hand over her mouth, and Dad would let his laugh-bark rip. I'd keep the one-liners coming until they were totally cracking up. By the end, they'd jump to their feet, applauding. For me.

That would mean everything.

Too bad it would never happen.

Or could it?

My brain whirls feverishly into motion.

Would it be such a crazy idea to invite my parents to the showcase? Granted, they'll go ballistic when they figure out that I've been lying to them. But maybe not. Maybe, just maybe, if I blow them away with my act like Jasmine said I would, they'll understand why I *had* to do it. Then they'll see why I need to go to PAMS.

But first, I have to convince my parents to listen with the one thing I can count on to get their attention: my education. From now on, I'll have to study extra hard so I can ace that stupid SSAT. I'll do whatever I have to do to prove to Mom and Dad that I can get good grades *and* do comedy at the same time. I don't need to go to a fancy school like Winston to ace standardized tests or get accepted into a "prestigious" college. I don't even know if I want to go to a "prestigious" college. I have to prove to them that I can do things my own way.

Yes. The hairs on my arm stand up. This might work.

For the first time since I started camp, I feel a bolt of confidence shoot through me.

A storm of thoughts spiral around as I rack my brain. I don't know exactly how I'm going to pull this off. All I know for sure is if I want a shot at going to PAMS, I have to give it all I've got.

I open to a blank page of my notebook and start plotting the details of Operation Show-My-Case.

OPERATION SHOW-MY-CASE

Who: Mom and Dad

What: Trick Mom and Dad to come see me perform at the Haha Club Comedy Camp Showcase

When: August 13

Where: Haha Club

Why: So they'll see my passion and talent for comedy and transfer me to PAMS

STEP ONE: Trick parents into going to the showcase

-Tell them it's a karaoke contest. Dad will care, Mom won't.

-Tell them it's where Yuri's secret boyfriend works. Mom will care, Dad won't.

-Tell them I'm getting an award for hagwon.

Explain that Mrs. Pak is having an awards ceremony for her top students at the new venue next to the library. (Do not mention it's called the Haha Club!)

STEP TWO: Perform my best material at the showcase

-Come up with and perfect my top jokes.

-Mom and Dad will watch me perform.

-They will be very confused but impressed.

-Tell them the truth about camp.

-Tell Jasmine about it, too.

STEP THREE: Ace the SSAT

-Study every night at least three hours after dinner.

-Ask Mrs. Pak for extra homework and additional practice tests. (Gulp!)

STEP FOUR: PAMS

-Ask Mom and Dad to let me audition for PAMS; they'll say yes because it's free and because of the showcase.

-Attend PAMS with Sienna and Felipe, get great grades, become world-class comedian.

Live happily <u>ever after.</u>

Me: Want to hear a joke?

Me: What's a Korean parent's favorite pastry?

Me: The HONOR ROLL! 🍞A⁺

Me: c'mon, that was funny

Me: . . .

Me: Yuri, you can't give us the silent treatment forever

Me: I know you secretly miss me to pieces

Me: Hello?

Me: you're really going to keep ignoring me?

Me: Fine. Be like that, then

CHAPTER 13

Felipe, Sienna, and I are hanging out in the Haha Club lobby after Jasmine dismisses us from camp a little early.

"Hey, are you going on the nursing home field trip with Jasmine tomorrow?"

"Yep, I'll be there," Sienna says, uncapping a purple Sharpie. "Sounds fun."

Felipe says, "Me too. What about you, Kay?"

Now that I know they're going to be there, I'll have to find a way to go . . . I just haven't figured out that part yet. "I'll try to make it."

Suddenly, Felipe's phone goes off.

"Oh, hey! Do you know what today is?" He bounces his eyebrows up and down and doesn't wait for us to answer. "Today is the day the new Beetleman comes out!" He says this with jazz hands.

"Who's that?" Sienna looks up from her elaborate

flower designs she's drawn across the front of her Converse.

He draws back in disbelief. "You don't know who Beetleman is?"

Sienna shakes her head.

"Nope, never heard of him," I say. From the sound of it, I'm not sure I want to. Beetles are basically my least favorite living thing, and I'd be totally fine if they all went extinct. But a man-sized beetle? I don't know if I can support that. Still, I'm kind of curious.

"Then you guys haven't *lived*. Come with me, friends. Allow me to introduce you two to the wonder that is Beetleman!"

I check the time. I still have fifteen whole minutes before I need to meet Mom at the library parking lot. "Sure, why not?"

Felipe leads us next door to Comic Underworld. I've peered through the windows once or twice, but I've always been too intimidated to enter. Let's just say it's not the most user-friendly store. First of all, it's laid out like an intricate maze in what feels like someone's garage, complete with obscure indie-rock music blaring from the speakers. The aisles consist of floor-to-ceiling shelves that are jam-packed with cardboard boxes of comic books. There are banners and signs labeling the genres: METACOMICS, PANTOMIME, FUMETTI NERI. Which are not at all helpful. They sound more like terms that would be on my vocab lists at Mrs. Pak's.

"This way, my ladies." Felipe heads straight back to the superhero section. He has definitely been here before. Then he stops abruptly. "Behold!" he says, waving his arms like a magician.

I look over his shoulder to see what the fuss is all about, and Sienna and I collapse into a hysterical fit of giggles.

OMG! Beetleman looks *exactly* like Felipe. Right down to his long sideburns and curly hair and everything.

"Why didn't you tell us you're the star of a comic book series?" Sienna holds the issue right next to his head to show the side-by-side resemblance.

"It's freakish," I admit, my eyes bouncing back and forth. "Felipe, he's your doppelganger," I say.

He studies the picture with new eyes. "No way. I'm much better-looking."

Spurred by Felipe's find, Sienna starts digging through the bins with the same fervor as my mom plowing through clearance racks. "I wonder if they've got one that looks like me," she says.

"I doubt they'll have an Asian girl one." I pick through a box on the low table. "They never have Asian anything."

Even the Japanese manga bin is filled with mostly blond-haired, huge-eyed girls.

Out of nowhere, there's a gasp from behind me.

It's Sienna. Her eyes meet mine, and she lifts a comic book with both hands slowly. "Look," she whispers.

Felipe pivots on his heel and says, "What the . . ." under his breath.

My jaw drops. "You're Chameleon Girl!"

"What kind of sorcery is this, Felipe?" she asks, flipping through the pages. "I mean, what are the odds we'd both find superheroes that look just like us?"

Chameleon Girl has got the same freckles, big hair, and long skinny limbs. And, to top it off, her superpower is the ability to change colors to blend in with her environment. It's uncanny.

"That's it." I plow back into my bin with a renewed sense of mission. "I've got to find mine, too."

"I know." Felipe scoots over a few rows and rifles through the stacks until he finds the one he's looking for.

"Here." He hands me a comic book from the anime section.

Sienna watches me for my reaction.

I burst out laughing when I see a busty ninja girl wearing a tight kimono and brandishing a huge samurai sword on the cover.

"Not even! C'mon, she's not me. She's Japanese!" Geez, why does everyone always think all Asians are the same?

"I thought you were Japanese." Felipe gives me a funny look. "Nakamura . . . That's a Japanese last name, right?"

The tips of my ears burn, and my mouth goes bone-dry.

"Yes, it is. You're right." I force a chuckle. "My name is Japanese, and so am I. Yup," I continue, instantly recognizing how stupid I sound. "What I meant was, I, Kay Nakamura, though I am of Japanese descent, am not a ninja. Yes, that's what I was trying to say."

"And I'm not really a chameleon," Sienna says with pursed lips, smelling my steaming hot pile of phoniness from a mile away.

"Or a beetle." Felipe thumps his puffed-up chest and then winces from the impact.

"The truth is," I cough out the words, scrambling for what to say next. "I don't understand why girl super-heroes are drawn this way. I mean, who really has pro-portions like that?"

Both of their heads snap back to take a second look at the comic book.

Felipe's ears turn sundubu red, and Sienna giggles, breaking the tension. "You know what, she needs more support to run and jump and kick butt." She gestures to her chest area with cupped hands. "At least that's what my mom says."

"C'mon, let's get going," Felipe says, like he's trying to change the subject. "My dad will be here any minute."

We head outside just as Mom's tan minivan pulls into the parking lot between the library and the comic book store.

Honk! Honk!

She rolls down the window and unlocks the door. "Ready to go?"

"Yup." I hope against hope that she won't ask about my new friends. But alas, her eyes immediately zero in on them.

"Who are your new friends?" She looks them up and down from behind her oversized aviator sunglasses.

"This is Sienna and Felipe." I don't need her knowing any more about them than that.

"Hello," they say at the same time.

"Nice to meet you, Mrs. Nak—"

"Mom!" I blurt out, cutting Felipe off before he has a chance to finish. "I'm hungry. Like, really hungry. What are we having for dinner? Bibimbap?" I hate to use Mom's penchant for feeding me against her, but I'm desperate.

Felipe shoots me a look I can't quite read.

Mom's face brightens. "I can make for you, if you want bibimbap."

"The kind with the long brown stuff?" I open the car door and hop inside.

"Okay, but we have to go to Korean market, then,"

Mom says, suddenly distracted. "We are out of gosari namul." She checks the time on her phone. "Oh! We should hurry before too much traffic. Nice to meet you, kids," she says, before she puts the car in reverse.

"Bye!" I yell to them, raising the car window as fast as I can.

Dodged a bullet there.

As we're pulling away, Mom asks, "Why did that boy call me Mrs. Nak?"

I answer quickly, "Oh, that? *Nak* probably means 'friend's mom' or something in Spanish. He's bilingual."

Mom nods slowly as she drives.

I can't tell if she's buying it or not.

"Those kids are students at Winston? I do not remember their faces."

Shoot, what do I say? I can't tell her they're from Winston. Knowing Mom, she'd try to look them up in the student directory to snoop. "Nope, uh. I know Sienna and Felipe from . . . er, hagwon."

Hagwon? Really, Yumi? Really?

"Those kids go to a Korean hagwon?" Mom looks at me warily with one hand on the wheel.

"Yes." My heart is speeding, but I have to go with it. What other choice do I have? I keep my voice and my eyeballs controlled the way I learned to do for the skits at camp.

"Haven't you heard? Mrs. Pak has been recruiting kids from the middle school to be peer tutors." It actually sounds halfway convincing the way it rolls off my tongue. "She selects only the most advanced kids with top grades and pays them to tutor us in study groups." I close my eyes and inhale deeply for effect. "I hope I get to be a peer tutor someday. Maybe if I study extremely hard . . ."

My delivery is downright Oscar-worthy.

"Advanced?" Mom's eyebrows do that furrow thing. "They must be such smart kids if Mrs. Pak pays them to work at top hagwon."

"Yeah, they're already learning trigonometry." I don't know why I added that. There was no need.

"Trigonometry?" Mom's head tilts to the side. She pauses a moment. "You should hang around with those kids, Yumi. Maybe they can help you with your work, and you can join the advanced group, too."

"Actually"—while I have her on my good side, I might as well push my luck—"Felipe and Sienna invited me to do some volunteer work with them tomorrow. Visiting the people in the nursing home, the one near the library. For community service. Really great on college applications. Can I go?"

"I like that idea. I can drop you off before work."

"Perfect!" I say, practically pinching myself. That was way easier than I thought it'd be.

"Much better to help the seniors than waste time with the comedy nonsense." Mom elbows me teasingly. "I see you are growing up and making mature choices."

"Thanks." I drop my head back onto the car headrest, and guilt gnaws at me from the inside. I don't know how much longer I can keep this up, but I have to. Just until the showcase.

CHAPTER 14

The next morning, I join my friends among the campers gathered in front of the nursing home right as Jasmine is going over some last-minute tips.

"Listen, there's going to be all kinds of folks who live in this facility," she explains as she unloads a few microphones and speakers from her car parked along the curb.

"Some are going to be more responsive than others. Just remember that your humor can bring a lot of joy, so don't be intimidated by the unfamiliar. Just be yourself."

We help her carry the equipment inside.

"Do you realize that this will be our first time performing outside of the Haha Club?" Sienna says, straightening her pink velvet cowboy hat. "This is going to be so next level! I'm totally nervous. Are you?"

"A little, to be honest," Felipe says.

"Me too." Even though I practiced seven of my strongest jokes in front of my laptop for almost an hour last night, I still feel unprepared.

The automatic glass door slides open, and we follow Jasmine into the lobby, where the walls are lined with dingy floral paintings and bulletin boards, like the kind we had in elementary school. The sign above the reception desk reads GREEN MEADOWS RESIDENTIAL FACILITY, but the harsh fluorescent lighting and that distinct hospital smell don't quite give off that green meadow feeling. More like green mildew, if you ask me.

We're herded into the common room while Jasmine sets up the audio stuff in the front stage area. There are maybe thirty or so senior citizens seated on chairs upholstered in vinyl. Some smile at us sweetly, some chat among themselves in wheelchairs, and some are staring off into space, unaware that we're even there. The nurses and caretakers in pastel scrubs lead the group in applause when Jasmine taps the microphone.

She greets them in her great big voice. "Good afternoon, ladies and gentlemen. My name is Jasmine Jasper, and today our young comedians from the Haha Club down the street will be performing a very special comedy show just for you. Let's give them a warm welcome!"

For the next half hour, I watch my fellow campers take the stage while trying in vain to rein in my jitters.

Sienna goes on and does this whole routine about how she's so overscheduled with extracurricular activities that her pets don't recognize her anymore.

When it's Felipe's turn, he does a bit about the advantages of being a chubby superhero and how he can fit more gadgets on his utility belt.

I watch one act after another, reminding myself that today is crucial for helping me narrow down which material I want to use for the showcase and audition. If I want to impress my parents, I have to pay attention to perfecting every detail. My pacing. My body positioning. My volume. All of it.

Just then, Jasmine calls my name.

I run up to the front and grab the microphone from the stand, taking care to stand up straight and fully face the audience. "Thank you, one more time for

Jasmine Jasper!" I say with my arm extended, just the way I practiced at home.

When the applause dies down, I launch in.

"I wish my parents were more relaxed like my friend's. She has the coolest parents. They let her do whatever she wants and wear whatever she wants. She doesn't have curfews, and she stays up late to watch R-rated movies. She once complained that they keep signing her up for so many acting classes to 'foster her creative spirit,'" I say with finger quotes. "The only thing my strict parents want to foster is a four-point-oh GPA."

I get a smattering of courtesy laughs.

No biggie. I'll get them with the next one.

I remind myself to walk. I am not a plant.

"Last week I was explaining to my immigrant parents how my friends get paid for each A they get on their report cards."

I wait a beat.

And then I drop the punch line.

"My dad looked me square in the eye and said, 'Should I also pay the dog to poop?'"

I get nothing. Just stone-cold silence.

The man in the front row loudly whispers to the lady next to him, "That's really harsh."

No one laughs, instead they start murmuring, and I hear phrases like "tiger parents" and "abusive."

Oh no, they've got it all wrong! My parents aren't like that; Dad was just trying to be funny.

Suddenly my throat is dry, and I can hear my pulse in my ears.

"Uh . . . so . . ."

There's a really awkward stretch of silence as I struggle to move on with my next joke, but I can't. I'm stuck.

Right then, Jasmine steps up to the mic and puts me out of my misery.

"Let's give it up one more time for Kay Nakamura!"

I slink off to my seat, ashamed that I'm toast after only two jokes. My mind reels with the million things I could have said or done differently to avoid that disaster. No matter what, I cannot bomb like this at the showcase. I have to deliver laughs—big laughs—if I want to convince Mom and Dad to let me audition for PAMS. The pressure crushes down on me so hard, I'm not sure I can stand up beneath it.

Soon enough, the show is over, and we head out front to wait for our parents to pick us up.

"That was absolutely brutal," I mutter to my friends.

"At least it's behind us," Felipe says.

"Easy for you to say. You finished your set." Unlike me, the only camper Jasmine had to bail out.

I turn to Sienna, but she doesn't say anything; she won't even look at me.

"What's wrong?" I ask her.

She blinks hard. "I didn't exactly appreciate you using my family as the butt of your joke."

I'm stunned. "What? No, you weren't the butt of my joke. I was. My parents were. Really! I was saying how jealous I am of you."

She turns her back to me. "That's not how it came across to me."

I look to Felipe, but he stays quiet.

"Sienna, I didn't mean to hurt your feelings. Honestly. I was only trying to be funny."

She jams her hands in her pockets. "Whatever, let's just drop it."

Right then, Jasmine calls from behind me, "Kay, can you help me take this equipment to my car?"

"Sure." Relieved to get away, I run over and grab the microphone stand and the bundle of cords from the ground and follow her to the side parking lot. I should be thrilled for some extra one-on-one time with her, but I'm too upset to fully appreciate it right now.

Jasmine probably senses it because she asks me, "Are you still thinking about your set?"

"Yeah, it definitely did not go as intended," I say, too sore to hide my feelings.

"It happens to the best of us. Don't beat yourself up over it." She balances a cardboard box on her hip as she fishes her car keys from her purse. "Who knows? Next time you might get a Tutti-Fruitti Jelly Belly."

"Huh?" Jelly Belly? What on earth . . .

"The Tutti-Fruitti Jelly Belly," she repeats, looking at me like what she's saying indeed makes sense. "You know how when you get a pack of Jelly Bellies, it's a mixed bag. You get the okay flavors like bubblegum and banana. Some awful ones like buttered popcorn and licorice. But when you get your favorite one, it makes having to get through all the bad and mediocre ones worth it. For me, it's all about the Tutti-Fruitti one."

Yeah, no. "I'm sorry, but I still don't know what you're talking about."

She opens the trunk of her lime green hatchback.

"Listen, what I'm trying to say is comedy is like that. You can't know which jokes work until you try them. And when you do, they're not all going to be great. Some will be decent. A few will be so bad you'll retch. But every now and then, you discover a winner—your favorite Jelly Belly. And that's what we comedians live for."

"You mean the Comedian's High?"

"Exactly." Jasmine places the cardboard box in the trunk, and I lay the microphone stand on its side next to it.

"If you think about it, your set today was more of a root beer jelly bean. And that could have been due to a number of factors. Might have been the crowd, might have been your wording. Doesn't mean that it's a bad joke. It just means it's not ready yet. You have to keep tweaking it."

"There's no fixing that set. It's a dud. Total failure."

She slams her trunk shut and leans on the bumper. "Well, most jokes start off as failures. It tells you what isn't working, which is a very valuable thing. Living with 'failure,'" Jasmine says with air quotes, "is an essential part of being a comedian."

I smirk. Mom and Dad sure would have some colorful opinions about that.

"You think I'm joking, but I'm not. I live with failure every day," she says. "Even now."

"What do you mean? You're a YouTube star with tens of thousands of fans and a comedy camp. That's not failure."

She starts laughing. "If only you knew. I teach at the Haha Club and online to help kids and to pay my bills, but you better believe I'm still out there pounding the pavement. I want to be a writer for kids' TV shows. I'm not there yet. In fact, this year alone I got passed over for two comedy writing gigs—one for a show on Cartoon Network and the other for Disney XD—but I keep hustling."

"Oh."

"I don't let these setbacks stop me, probably because I can't help it. I love to make people laugh." She winks at me. "What can I say? I'm a sucker for the Tutti-Fruitti Jelly Bellies."

I smile.

We head back to the front of the nursing home, and all the campers have been picked up. "Thanks for your help with the equipment. I'll wait with you until your parents come," she offers.

"No, it's fine. I'm taking the bus. The stop is really close."

"Okay, then. Think about what we talked about. Failure is your friend!" she says before we part.

I walk over to the bus stall around the corner.

It's true, I do really appreciate her whole get-back-up-again message and everything, but she'll never understand the world I'm coming from—the same way I don't understand her world or Sienna's. Let's be real: my situation is different. I can't afford to fail over and over like they can. I literally have one chance to convince my parents that I should pursue comedy at PAMS, and all the jelly bean flavors on the planet won't help me with that.

CHAPTER 15

It's Sunday before lunch service, and I'm helping Dad install the new disco ball he ordered from the internet.

"Feels good for construction to be finished," Dad says, climbing up the ladder. "Look at this stage. Isn't it great?"

"I have to admit, it's really cool." The soft lighting on the raised wooden platform fills out the entire back area, giving our restaurant a cozy focal point.

"Karaoke will be a hit with the new customers." He grabs a heavy-duty power tool from his leather holster. "It will bring back good fortune for our family."

It's a relief to see him smile again. He hasn't talked about it much to me, but it's clear by the way he stomps around the restaurant that he's still upset about how things went down with Yuri.

Earlier today, I overheard him talking to Manuel. "Twenty years I raised her, but she will not even answer my phone calls. So ungrateful!" Which only got Manuel going about his teenage niece, who barely looks up from her phone when he comes home from work. Luckily, their little vent session broke when the workers finally finished up construction. He's been distracted by getting the stage ready ever since. This is the best mood I've seen him in in days.

"So how does this disco ball work?" I ask Dad.

He perks up. "Let me show you." He hits a button on the remote and the sparkly globe glitters as it rotates, dappling the wall of traditional brush paintings with festive dots of lights.

I hoist myself up onstage.

"Oooooh, it really transforms the place!" I spin around with my arms outstretched. "I feel like I'm on *American Idol.*"

"Right?" He leans the ladder against the wall and admires the disco ball.

I grip the microphone from the stand. "Ladies and gentlemen, the multitalented restaurateur-slash-singer superstar . . . Mr. Bong Ju Chung!"

My dad, the ultimate karaoke king, cannot refuse the

microphone. He takes it in both hands and belts out his go-to song, an old classic Korean folk a cappella.

"Ho-rang nabi han maree gaaaaaaa ggot baht-te anjan-undeeeeeee," he sings in perfect pitch.

"I thought it wasn't good to show off." I giggle.

"Who is showing off? This is just how I sing. I cannot help," Dad says, playing dumb.

Mom rolls her eyes as she plops into an empty booth with a cardboard box in her arms.

"You two stop being foolish and help me. Mr. Montgomery is going to be here soon."

She says it sternly, but the corners of her eyes turn up warmly as she rolls plastic utensils and disposable chopsticks into napkin bundles for today's to-go orders.

"I dedicate this song to my best-dressed wife, who makes most delicious food in Koreatown." Then he croons a Korean love song, showing off his silky tenor.

Mom runs her fingers through her hair. "Aigoo cham-nah." Which means something similar to "oh, come on, now." Dad's romancing seems to be working, because pretty soon, Mom is clapping along with the beat as he sings.

My parents' lovey-dovey mood is cute, but only in small doses. Like wasabi. If they don't cut it out soon, they're going to make me lose my lunch.

Dad takes a dramatic bow after his song finishes. "See? This stage is already bringing joy back to our restaurant. It will sound even better when we get the big speakers."

Mom waves us over. "Now come help me finish this."

I join her in the booth and start bundling.

"Dad, when's the new audio stuff going to be put in?"

He smiles broadly. "They are coming this Wednesday. We have to close restaurant so they can install, but it will be worth it."

I knew any mention of the audio equipment would keep him in good spirits. He's one of those people who can tinker with the bass and treble dials on a stereo system forever until he gets the purest sound. He's the only Korean dad I know who rocks the Beats by Dre headphones.

"I ordered the top-of-the-line speakers," he says, rattling off all the features that make no sense to me or anyone outside of Best Buy.

"That's great, Dad." I grab another handful of plastic spoons. "What about publicity for the Grand Reopening? You know, how are we going to spread the word?"

"Aha! I will show you." Dad goes over and unboxes the newly printed posters for the big event. "I got these made. I will post them at every church and restaurant in Koreatown."

Hmm. Churches and competing restaurants don't sound like the most obvious places to attract new diners.

"Oh, I have an idea." I pull out my phone. "We should create an Instagram account and post a Facebook event, too. The hashtag 'ktown' is popular. A lot of food writers and social media influencers—"

"Omo omo," Mom interrupts, pushing the phone from my hands. "Put that away. You don't know what kind people are on internet."

"We don't need," Dad says. "We have these posters, and I already put ad in Korean newspaper."

He slides the posters back into the box.

"But what about the people who don't read the Korean newspaper?" I ask. "How are they going to hear about Chung's Barbecue and Karaoke?"

"What are you talking about?" Mom secures a rubber band to her bundle. "Everybody reads the Korean newspaper."

Uh. No, the waygookin most certainly don't, but I don't want to argue with her and ruin this moment.

Then Mom's phone chimes loudly from her purse on the hostess stand. She gets up to answer it. "Hello?" Her back straightens when she hears the voice on the other end. "Oh yes, how are you, Mrs. Pak?"

Mrs. Pak? I break into a cold sweat, the plasticware slipping from my hands.

Why is she calling my mother?

As I scramble to retrieve the fallen cutlery, I strain my ears to catch bits of their conversation. Mom paces around mm-hmming a few times. "Our Yumi did that?" she says in an almost whisper. I can't tell if it's good news or bad news. Oh shoot, did Mrs. Pak find out I've been sneaking off to the Haha Club? I hold my breath. If there's anyone who would find out, it'd be her. Mrs. Pak knows everything. She's calling to rat me out, I just know it. My life flashes before my very eyes.

"Thank you so much for calling me," Mom says graciously. "Yes, goodbye."

I hold my breath, preparing for the worst.

"What did Mrs. Pak want?" asks Dad, who's also hovering over her.

Mom pauses. "She called to tell me Yumi is studying hard and improved on her practice test the other day. She got the ninety-two percent."

"What?" I'm straight-up slack-jawed.

Hallelujah!

Mrs. Pak doesn't know about my secret. I'm not busted. I'm not going to die. *And* my tests are improving exactly according to plan.

"Score is not there yet, but at least you are making progress." Mom shakes a finger at me. "You need to study more to reach goal, okay?"

"Yes, Mom."

I know it doesn't sound anything like a compliment—in fact it probably sounds more like scolding— but I know what she's saying: she's pleased. My mother is the type who is unable say something encouraging without attaching some kind of warning to balance it out. Like when she tells me, "You are pretty, but if you don't put on sunscreen, your skin will turn rough like dried squid." It's just her way, but I can read between the lines.

It occurs to me that this is the perfect moment to initiate Operation Show-My-Case, while I have them on my good side.

—Tell them I'm getting an award for hagwon.

Explain that Mrs. Pak is having an awards ceremony for her top students at the new venue next to the library. (Do not mention it's called the Haha Club!)

"So, Mom, Dad, I have something very important to tell you," I start to say.

Dad glances at the time. "Okay, but hurry up. We have a meeting at eleven o'clock."

I take a deep breath. "So, there's this special awards ceremony—"

"Award?" Mom repeats with a glimmer in her eye. "What kind award? From hagwon?"

But then there's some knocking at the door.

"It's me," a deep voice calls. "Lloyd."

"He's early." Dad nearly falls out of the booth as he scrambles to unlock the door. "Mr. Montgomery, please come in."

Mr. Montgomery, or, as my parents pronounce it, Mr. Mongle-merry, is the guy who owns the strip mall where our restaurant is located. Every time I see him, he gives me a lollipop like I'm a little kid.

"Well, if it isn't Yumi," he says as he steps inside. "You've grown so much since the last time I saw you." He lets out a hearty laugh, pulling a lime-flavored Dum-Dum from the front pocket of his cracked leather briefcase.

"Thank you."

What is this meeting about, anyway?

Mom gives me a look, and I take my cue to make myself scarce by holing up in the kitchen, peeking through the crack in the door.

"Good to see you again, Mr. Montgomery!" Dad says.

"Bong, please." Mr. Montgomery shakes his hand. "I've been telling you for fifteen years, call me Lloyd."

My dad says it like he's trying not to swallow his tongue. This man's name is seriously a native Korean speaker's worst nightmare.

"Welcome, would you like some tea?" Mom asks, clearing the table of the to-go utensils.

"No, thank you." He straightens his necktie. "I won't be here long."

I watch as Dad leads Mr. Montgomery to an empty table. "How can I help you?"

He removes his well-worn cap. "You've been my tenant for a long time, and I've enjoyed doing business with you." He scratches the back of his neck. "So this isn't easy for me to say . . ."

Just say it already.

"But I'm under a lot of pressure . . . You're two months behind on rent." He coughs into his fist. "Bong, you know I consider you my friend, but I can't let it slide anymore."

My muscles contract. Obviously, we were having financial problems, but I had no idea that it was this bad.

"I'm sorry, Mr. Montgomery," Dad pleads, searching the tabletop like he's looking for his dignity.

My father is not one to apologize. Especially not like that.

He bows his head in shame like a little boy getting scolded by his father. "The construction cost for renovation was more than budget."

"Please, sir. We just need a little more time. Our Grand Reopening is this Saturday," Mom begs.

With that, to my great relief, Dad regains his posture.

He stands up beside the table. "Yes, that's right. We are having our Grand Reopening, and we are gonna pay back all the past-due amount." He walks a few paces and gestures to the brand-new karaoke stage behind him. "Just a few more days, and we will have the money for you."

Mr. Montgomery takes a look around the place, noticing the new stage for the first time. "I sure hope so, Bong," he says with a resigned sort of smile. "Because that new Pilates studio next door is interested in expanding into this space, and if you can't make rent, I'm going to have to explore that option."

Mr. Montgomery puts his cap back on his bald head. "I can only give you eight more days to get on track," he says solemnly. "Good luck."

Dad grabs Mr. Montgomery's hand with both of his and shakes it vigorously, jostling the old man like a rag doll. "Thank you, Mr. Montgomery. You can count on me."

Mom shakes his hand, too. "Please have a good day."

After the door closes and Mr. Montgomery is gone, Mom collapses into the booth.

"Don't worry, yobo," Dad reassures her softly in Korean, massaging her shoulders. "Trust me. Uncle from San Jose can give us a loan, and we can make the rest at the Grand Reopening. This is no problem. We will be okay."

But will we?

That's a lot of money to make in such a short span.

For the first time in my life, I think my parents might be in over their heads.

There's a lump the size of a disco ball lodged in my throat.

We need help.

Me: Yuri, text me, it's urgent

Me: I'm not joking around

Me: Stuff's happening with mom and dad at the restaurant

Me: money stuff

Me: I think it's a big deal

Me: I'm starting to get really worried

Me: I mean it, Yuri. I'm not making this up

Me: I need to talk to you

Me: Yuri?

CHAPTER 16

I'm on a bus bound for UCLA a few hours later.

I've had enough of Yuri's silent treatment. If she isn't going to answer her phone, I'll have to talk to her in person.

This is serious.

Except getting to her is turning out to be much harder than I thought it'd be.

"Finding a Starbucks should not be this difficult," I mutter.

After circling the sprawling UCLA medical school campus in ninety-five degree heat for more than an hour, past huge brick libraries and modern high-rises, through rolling lawns, and up and down an untold number of stairs, I am seriously sweaty, tired, and just plain over it.

The GPS is draining my battery, so I close out my

map app on my phone. I'm this close to calling it quits and going back to Koreatown where I'm supposed to be when I finally spot it.

Across the street, in the window of a huge building, there's a tiny sign that blinks COFFEE.

No wonder I couldn't find it! It's not even a normal Starbucks—it's more like a dinky coffee cart on the main floor that PROUDLY SERVES STARBUCKS.

I wipe away the beads of perspiration dotting my forehead and cross the street.

The doors part, and I immediately scan the expansive air-conditioned lobby in search of Yuri.

There are two people working the counter.

Wait, is that her?

I draw closer to get a better look.

It's jarring. My sister, who Mom once described to some customers as the Asian Audrey Hepburn, perfectly poised in pastel cardigans and tasteful ballet flats, is wearing an apron and a floppy logoed baseball cap, making a drink.

She freezes when her eyes meet mine.

"Yumi, what are you doing here?"

"I, um, had to talk to you, and you weren't return-ing my texts," I stammer, reminding myself to hold my ground. I knew it was going to be a bold move to show up at her work unannounced, but I had no other choice.

I need her.

"How did you even get here?"

Her tone is terse.

"I took the bus." I shrug casually like I didn't spend forever on Google Street View researching my trek across Los Angeles to get here. Some help that was.

"The bus? By yourself?" Yuri's eyes bulge.

"Well, me and Siri," I joke.

"Do Mom and Dad know you're here?"

"No . . . they think I'm at Ginny's." I fidget with the loose thread on my backpack strap.

Right then, a petite lady in a gold pantsuit waves her arm wildly at my sister from the beverage pickup area.

"Excuse me, miss. I ordered a decaf soy latte with an extra shot and cream." She takes the tiniest sip and wrinkles her Barbie nose. "Yeah. You made this with almond milk. You need to make me a new one," she says with a smile that isn't a smile at all. "Now."

She plops her Venti cup back on the counter. Yuri and her bearded coworker exchange glances as if they're deciding who is going to deal with her.

"We'll be right with you, ma'am." Yuri unties her apron. "Hey, Bruce, sorry to do this to you, but something came up that I urgently need to take care of. Is it okay if I take my break early?"

Bruce checks his watch. "Fine, but only ten minutes, okay?" he says with a tight smile.

Disgruntled Pantsuit Lady drums her French manicured fingers on the counter dramatically. "Excuse me?"

"Bruce will take care of you." Yuri leads me outside to the courtyard, where there's a bench next to a huge fountain.

"What's going on? Is everything okay?"

I get straight to the point. There's no reason to beat around the bush.

"It's the restaurant. We're in trouble." I fill her in on all the details of Mr. Montgomery's visit. About the two months of missed rent. About the eight days we have to get it all back.

She sits there a moment with her arms crossed and a blank expression on her face.

"Well, aren't you going to say anything?" I search her face for something. Anything. But there's nothing. The only sound comes from the water sploshing from the nearby fountain.

"You came all the way here while *I'm working* to tell me *that*?" She tucks a stray strand behind her ear. This was not the reaction I was expecting. "I'm not sure what you thought I was going to tell you."

A flash of anger burns my cheeks. "You're supposed to help fix this."

Why is she acting like she doesn't care we could very well lose the restaurant in a matter of days? Like this isn't her problem, too.

She takes a deep breath. "I'm sure Mom and Dad know what they're doing. We have to trust this Grand Reopening karaoke thing will be a success."

"That's it? That's all you have to say?"

If I'd known Yuri was going to blow me off like this, I wouldn't have wasted hours of my time wandering all around freaking UCLA in search of her advice.

"Look, it's not like I'm a genie who can solve all our family's problems."

"Apparently." I turn away so I don't have to look at her. "All you care about is leaving us to join the stupid Peace Corps." My throat aches with repressed tears. "You don't know about anything that's going on with me, since you can't be bothered to return my texts . . ."

"Yumi, that's not fair." Her voice softens. "You know I've had a lot going on."

I don't even want to hear it.

"Well, for your information, so have I. Not that you'd care. You're too *busy* with your new life to know how stressed out I've been about the showcase this Thursday," I say coolly, with resentment I didn't know I had.

"What showcase?" Her head jerks, suddenly confused.

I panic, realizing my mistake. I'm so used to Yuri knowing everything about my life, I forgot to leave out the camp stuff.

"The one at comedy camp . . ." I say, my lip twitching.

"You got Mom and Dad to sign you up for comedy camp?"

There's a moment of awkward silence.

"Yumi . . ." she scolds me, sounding exactly like Mom.

This is bad. Very, very bad. It's too late for me to back-track now. I have no choice but to come clean.

Big mistake.

"What? No!" Yuri snaps. "Do you mean to tell me that you've been pretending to be Kay this whole time? Behind Mom and Dad's back?" She sucks in her breath. "Yumi, what were you thinking?"

I double down. "This was your idea! You're the one who told me I needed to pursue comedy. Remember? If I don't go for it, I'll be chasing Mom and Dad's dreams, not my own. Those were your words, not mine."

"But I never told you to lie and pretend to be some-one else." Yuri's eyes laser beam into me. "Have you considered that someone somewhere is paying for Kay to go to comedy camp? Not you? That's like stealing. Do you realize that?"

I hesitate, the words jamming up in my mouth. "Well, I wasn't thinking about it like that. I thought it was des-tiny for me to meet Jasmine Jasper." I avert my eyes. "Anyway, it's not like I'm hurting anyone."

"No, Yooms. It doesn't work like that."

She flings open her purse and grabs her checkbook. "Listen to me. You need to fix this. You are going to go to the Haha Club tomorrow to tell Jasmine Jasper the truth. Then you will give her this check and apologize for your deception."

"But—"

Yuri's face is dead serious. "And then you're going to confess all of this to Mom and Dad."

It's right then that I lose it. I completely lose it. The thought of Mom and Dad finding out sends my body buckling into a sobbing fit. The little-kid kind with the snot and the red face and heaving breaths in front of all of Westwood to see. I've worked too hard for my plan to blow up now.

"Yuri. Please. I—I can't . . ." I say between ragged breaths, trying to brush off the curious looks I'm getting from people passing by. "They'll make me quit camp. Without ever seeing me perform. And they'll never send me to PAMS."

Then my life will be over, and I'll be back to being the easy target at Winston.

Yuri's face crumples, and she hands me a tissue from

her bag. She puts her arm around me. "Come on, don't cry, Yumi." I bury my head in my arms and let the crashing sound of the fountain drown out my blubbering.

I get myself together enough to tell her about Operation Show-My-Case. "I've been staying up past midnight every night studying my butt off to prove to them I can do this. So I can give them their ninety-eight percent," I explain, wiping my eyes. "Then maybe they'll take me seriously about comedy. You know how Mom and Dad are. They won't support something until they see it. Isn't that why you waited to tell us about the Peace Corps?"

She looks uncomfortably at her hands, avoiding my eyes.

I press further. "You kept the whole Peace Corps thing a secret from them until it was a done deal. You even kept it from me." My voice cracks.

"Yumi, I didn't want to. I just wasn't ready—"

"Neither am I. You of all people should understand why I need more time. Please, don't make me tell Mom and Dad yet," I plead.

There's a long pause.

Finally, she speaks. "Fine." She puts the check in my hands. "But I still want you to clear things up with Jasmine Jasper. It's the right thing to do. Promise me."

"Okay, I will." I take the check and tuck it away into my notebook pocket.

"By the way, that check is a loan." She taps my notebook with two fingers. "Just so you know, I'll have to work a bunch of extra shifts to cover this. I expect you to reimburse me in full as soon as you can."

"Okay." I sniff.

She nudges me with her elbow. "Look, let me see what I can do about the showcase. I'll ask Bruce if I can get that day off. Manuel and I will hold down the restaurant during the lunch rush so Mom and Dad can go."

I maul my sister in a giant bear hug. "Thank you, thank you, Yuri." But then I push my luck. "So does that mean you'll smooth things over with Mom and Dad?"

It's about time they settle things anyway.

Yuri relents. "I suppose."

"Great."

This will fix everything. Not only will Yuri make peace

with Mom and Dad, she'll also help me with Operation Show-My-Case. It'll be a win for everyone.

I can almost picture it now: Mom and Dad will be so impressed and overcome with emotion after my performance, they'll agree to send me to PAMS. Maybe Yuri will be so moved by all the love that she'll cancel her plans with the Peace Corps and decide to stay. Then we'll be one big happy family again.

I just need to get them to the showcase.

"What would I do without you?" I rest my head on hers.

She strokes my hair. "Yumi, you don't ever have to pretend to be anyone else, okay? You are enough just as you are," she tells me. "Now go fix this mess."

CHAPTER 17

I'm walking to the Haha Club and the butterflies in my belly are the size of vultures.

I check my phone again. Fifteen minutes before camp starts. Should be plenty of time.

I breathe in through my nose slowly.

Don't overthink this, Yumi. Simply tell Jasmine what happened, apologize, and give her the money. She is kind, and she'll understand. Chances are, we'll laugh about this whole thing by tomorrow.

I head inside, steeling myself for the encounter, just as Jasmine's voice floats in from the staff lounge.

Gulp.

It's now or never.

I knock softly on the door.

The door flings open. "Hey, Kay," Jasmine says with her phone to her ear.

My body temperature plummets. Now that we're face-to-face, my confidence drains from me like dishwater through a grease trap.

"I, uh, wanted to talk to you about something, but since you're on the phone . . ." My voice falters. "I can come back later."

She gestures for me to join her in the empty lounge. "Don't be silly. Come on in. I'll only be a minute. I'm on hold."

"Okay."

I follow her into the staff lounge.

To be honest, I've always wondered what it was like in here, but it's kind of anticlimactic. It's nothing but a plain, boring room with a huge conference table littered with paper piles, empty pizza boxes, Doritos bags, and soda cans. Not that I was expecting whoopee cushions and beanbag chairs, but this doesn't quite live up to the mystique.

"Ignore the mess. Comedians are such pigs." She wanders to the kitchen area. "Make yourself at home."

I sit down and get out my Super-Secret Comedy Notebook with Yuri's check inside the front flap. If only I could just throw it at her like a paperboy and run away.

Then I hear Jasmine say, "No, that's okay," into the phone. Her face shrivels in disgust. "What? You know I can't do that, Mark."

My ears perk.

She paces back and forth in the kitchen like a cat stalking a mouse hole. "I am not going to *sue* her. She's my former student!"

Sue? That sounds pretty serious. I look away and study the old promo posters that line the wall, trying not to eavesdrop. I recognize a bunch of famous comedians and some I don't know, too. They all stand in front of the same red velvet curtain, holding a microphone, doing a set. Living the dream.

"No, listen. There's got to be another way we can work this out." Jasmine glances in my direction. "Call me back when you get more information." She hangs up without saying goodbye and comes my way.

My heart bangs in my chest at warp speed.

"Thanks for waiting." She sits in a chair next to mine. "Important call from my lawyer. Legal stuff."

She sticks out her tongue and crosses her eyes like a dead toad.

I let out a nervous chuckle.

"So much drama today." Jasmine covers her eyes with both hands. "Apparently, a former student is stealing my jokes."

"Really?" What kind of monster would plagiarize her own teacher?

"Yeah, it's some hot-buttered nonsense."

"That does sound buttery. Er, nonsensical. I mean, bad." I'm not used to adults telling me their private business. I wonder if Jasmine can tell.

Jasmine has a bewildered look in her eyes, like she's wound up and needs to vent. "The red flags were everywhere, now that I think about it. She comes over to the club out of the blue to say hi, and after she leaves, my notebook has gone missing. And pretty soon videos start popping up all over the internet of her doing stand-up with my material. At first I thought it was a coincidence, because I didn't want to believe she was the one who took my notebook. But now it's crystal clear. She stole from me."

"Wow." This person has some gall. Everyone knows that notebooks are off-limits. Some things are sacred.

I hold tightly to my own notebook, the very one I started last year after watching Jasmine's *Improving Your Craft* vlog episode number four: "Recording Your Comedy Material."

If anyone ever stole it, I'd die. My obituary would read *Yumi Chung, age eleven, tragically perished from overembarrassment when her most intimate thoughts and dreams were read by others.*

"And to think, I was her mentor for three years . . . She shakes her head slowly.

"I'm sorry to hear that."

"What's worse is when I called her out, she had the nerve to deny it."

"She did?"

"Mm-hmm. Said it wasn't her." Jasmine grimaces. "After all the time and energy I'd invested in her, she *lied* to my face." She throws up her arms. "Lied!"

My fingernails dig into my thighs.

"That's the part I still can't get over." Her mouth bunches to the side in disdain. "Lord knows I try to be a forgiving person, but if there's one kind of person I cannot stand, it's liars."

Suddenly, the walls start closing in on me.

She looks directly at me. "You think you know some-one . . ."

I can't breathe.

"Sorry, I'm oversharing again." She leans in close to me. "Tell me, Kay, what did you come here to talk to me about?"

The sight of my comedy notebook in my lap makes me feel sick. Its scuffed cover and worn pages. The check is right there, right inside the flap. All I have to do is open it and give it to her.

But I can't.

I can't!

She'll know I'm a liar. Another liar she cannot stand.

She'll never forgive me. And she'll tell Mom and Dad, and they'll make me leave camp, and I'll lose everything.

I clear my throat, and against my better judgment, I do it again—I lie through my teeth. "I—I, uh . . . was going to ask you to write me a letter of recommendation for the Performing Arts Magnet School."

Jasmine's face lights up.

"Now, that's what I'm talking about!" She smiles. "I'm writing letters for Felipe and Sienna, too."

All I can do is shrug. I feel like scum. No, lower than scum. I feel like the sludge that comes from the scum's ears and armpits.

"Look at you, putting yourself out there. I'm so glad you're auditioning for this. Fear of failure is a real thing, but you're not letting it scare you anymore."

I want to cover my ears to block her out. I can't stand to hear her say one more nice thing about me. "No. Please . . . stop."

"You don't have to be so modest." Jasmine beams at me. "You deserve all the good Jelly Bellies, Kay."

I clench my teeth to keep from falling apart.

"You got this." The lightness in her voice pierces me with guilt. "I believe in you."

"Thank you," I mutter, getting to my feet.

"You're very welcome," she says warmly. "I'll have it ready for you tomorrow."

"Okay." I put my notebook back into my bag.

The check and the truth still in it.

MRS. PAK'S HAGWON

REACHING FOR IVY LEAGUE DREAMS

Midterm Progress Report

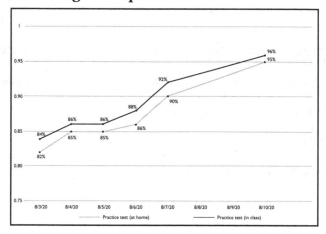

Comments: Yumi is making continued progress, she is beginning to participate more in class, and she is showing more confidence in her answers. She has been consistent with turning in her assignments.

Areas of Concern: Yumi needs to work on staying awake in class and take notes of only class-related matters.

Parent Signature _____ **Date** _____

CHAPTER 18

"If I don't eat something in the next four seconds, I'm going to die," Ginny says, dropping her backpack onto the table in the hagwon student lounge.

"I'm hungry, too." Well, I *was* until I unlatched my plastic bento box to find cold rice, kimchi, limp pickled cucumbers, and sad beef strips in soy sauce.

"Blech." I feel a prick of guilt for complaining, knowing Mom gets up early to make me these home-cooked lunches. I bet it was really tasty when she packed it, but now . . . not so much.

Ginny opens her own container, and she's got rice, soggy edamame soybean pods, floppy tofu rectangles, and, to her horror, Spam slices.

Okay, Ginny has it worse.

"Seriously, Spam? It's like she's gets her kicks by torturing me with these processed meat products. This is literally a vegan's worst nightmare! She might as well put some lard on top for garnish."

"Maybe she thinks it'll help you get taller," I joke.

"Well, she should know by now that this is the last thing on earth I'd ever want to eat." She pokes at it with her fork like it might come to life and eat her. "Cancel that. I'd rather starve to death.

"Wanna get tacos?" she suggests.

"Yes."

I feel bad dumping my lunch, but the taco truck around the corner is so cheap and delicious, it's impossible to say no.

I am practically salivating when I get my plate of tiny corn tortillas piled high with chopped onions, cilantro, and sizzling beef topped with a generous drizzle of spicy salsa verde and radish slices on the side. Ginny gets her usual vegan black bean torta.

We carry our trays over to the plastic lawn chairs set up in the shady corner of the parking lot. We're the only ones here today. Which works for me, because I want nothing more than to drown my troubles in Mexican food and not think about yesterday's botched confession attempt at the Haha Club.

I squeeze a lime wedge over my tacos and dive in as Ginny goes on and on about her mom and her vegan lifestyle. I'm licking my fingers when my phone vibrates in my pocket.

I put down my plate and reach for my phone.

Immediately, I break into a cold sweat.

There's a string of unopened text messages from Yuri.

Yuri: Did you tell Jasmine Jasper yet?

Yuri: How did it go?

Yuri: I checked my bank account, she hasn't cashed the check.

Yuri: You didn't do it yet, did you?

Yuri: Hello? Yumi?

Yuri: YUMI

Yuri: Why aren't you returning my texts?

Yuri: Are you trying to get back at me because I didn't reply to yours?

Yuri: I'm really sorry about that, btw

Yuri: Seriously though, I need you to follow through with this. It's the right thing to do.

Yuri: I hate to do this to you, but if you can't take responsibility, I'm going to have to talk to Mom and Dad.

Yuri: Call me

I panic.

Seriously, she's threatening to snitch on me now?

I should have known this might happen. Things were a little off last night when my sister came over to patch things up with Mom and Dad. I listened in from the top of the stairs for the whole hour as they talked in hushed voices in the living room. Yuri apologized for her disappearing act. Then Dad explained that while he doesn't agree with her quitting school, he'll support her decision to join the Peace Corps.

I was about to head back to my room after I thought a truce had been reached, but then Mom started confiding in Yuri about how concerned she was about me. How I've been so stressed and tired all the time. How I waste so much time on the computer and how she isn't sure if I'm going to get the scholarship. And Yuri just sat there and did not say one word to defend me. I swear, it was as if she was debating whether or not to tell them about what I've been up to at the Haha Club.

Some ally!

My whole life I've trusted Yuri with my secrets, and she's always been on my side, but I've never put her in a situation that required her to be my accomplice. This does not bode well for me, being that my sister is the world's biggest rule follower. She can't even get through a game of Monopoly without consulting the official directions a dozen times. Not to mention she's an adult and adults are prone to act irrationally when they're worried. And based on this thread of texts, Yuri is more than a little bit worried.

Terror grips me at the realization that my own sister, my own flesh and blood, might rat me out.

I drop my head into my hands. Then what'll I do?

Ginny puts down her torta. "Whoa, Yumi. Is everything okay?"

I wish I could say yes and play it off like everything is

fine, but it's too much. My plans are teetering like Jenga bricks, and I'm going to get caught under the rubble of my deception if I don't find a way out. Fast.

"What's the matter?"

So I tell Ginny. I tell her everything. It comes out in one piece, like a giant run-on sentence. The more I say, the more her face scrunches up like she's majorly constipated. I don't take a breath until it's all out. The whole ugly, twisted truth.

I cringe, waiting for her response.

"Yumi . . . that's a lot to take in," she finally says, which doesn't exactly give me the weight-off-my-shoulders feeling I was hoping for. She takes a swig from her Jarritos orange soda and pauses for another moment to absorb the horrific details of my dilemma.

"I don't know how I got caught up in it." I put down the half-eaten taco on my plate, my appetite suddenly gone.

"Ginny, if you were me, what would you do?" I ask desperately.

"Honestly?"

"Yeah."

"If I were you, I'd leave the check for Jasmine whatever-her-name-is at the club office and then never return."

My whole body lurches. Never return?

"What about the showcase? And my parents and PAMS? And the New Me?"

"I'd drop it. All of it," she says, unblinking.

"But . . . PAMS . . ."

"This is probably not what you want to hear right now." She dabs the sides of her mouth with a napkin. "But, c'mon. Winston is literally the best school around, and you're so close to getting the scholarship. Why would you consider giving that up?"

"Winston is not that great, Ginny. I've been there a whole year, remember?" Heat rises in my cheeks. "The kids . . . they're cliquey, and the teachers are demanding. It's stressful and lonely there. Sixth grade was the worst."

"But it'll get you into a good college," she says, sounding like my parents. "Your mom and dad aren't going to let you give that up to tell some jokes. No matter how well you do at this showcase thing."

"But Jasmine Jasper said that I'm talented and that I

have to keep working at it if I want to get the Tutti-Fruitti Jelly Bellies."

Ginny pauses for a moment as if she's searching for the right words.

"You totally lost me with the candy reference, but all I'm trying to say is Jasmine Jasper isn't Korean. She will never understand our parents." Ginny puts a hand on my shoulder. "Look at us. We can barely make sense of them, and they're *our parents.*"

"B-but—"

She puts up her hand. "I'm your friend, so I hate to say this, but I honestly think you need let the comedy thing go. Or at least put it on pause. That's what my brother is doing with his DJing. You can do it when you're in college or something."

My head jerks. College? That's a lifetime away. Is Ginny trying to say I'm not allowed to be happy until I'm eighteen?

"Have you thought realistically about how freaked out your parents would be if they found out you've been lying to them this whole time?"

Flashes of Dad yelling, red in the face, pop into my

head. I see Mom's thin lips pressed together in silent disappointment. Their matching horrified expressions burn in my mind.

"Why would you do this?" they'd ask me.

I search within myself for the answer to their question, and I still don't have one that'll satisfy them. How can I make them see that I'm not doing this to hurt them? I'm doing this because this is what I love to do.

Ginny is right, they'd never understand. Not in a million years.

"You know it, and I know it. They're *never* going to change their minds about the Winston thing."

I close my eyes. "What am I supposed to do, then?"

"Well." She takes another gulp of her drink. "Look on the bright side: they don't know anything yet. You should get out while you still can."

Her words ring in my ears.

Get out while you still can. Get out while you still can. Get out while you still can.

Later that night, I'm back in the restaurant office trying to go over my vocabulary flash cards, but I can't focus.

I'm too spooked by what Ginny said at lunch.

This whole time, I've been busting my butt running between hagwon and the Haha Club and the restaurant, trying to do it all. Practicing my jokes. Staying up late at night finishing my homework. Plus helping out at the restaurant. For what? For the hope that maybe my parents might finally see what a stellar daughter I am and agree to send me to PAMS?

What gave me the idea they'd ever do that in the first place? All they've ever cared about is me getting good grades and going to a good school. Nothing else matters to them. They're quick to tamp down on anything that takes away from my academics, especially anything "risky." And what is comedy? It's nothing but risk.

Did I really think a few funny lines would change all that? Since when have Mom and Dad ever listened to anything I had to say? Why would they start now?

I hurl my index cards onto the floor.

I should just quit. The sooner the better.

It's decided. Tomorrow after camp, I'll do like Ginny suggested. At dismissal, I'll slip Yuri's check into Jasmine

Jasper's bag and disappear forever. And that'll be the end of this whole fiasco.

Done and done.

I'm picking up my flash cards from the ground right as Manuel comes into the office.

He grabs his time card from the shelf. "How's it going?"

"You know, the usual," I reply, my voice noticeably flat.

His eyebrows collide in concern. "You got something on your mind?"

"Nothing much, you know, just my life is blowing up. That's all." I bury my head in my arms.

It's quiet for a moment.

"Things will turn around," he says.

"Manuel, what would you do if you had to choose between making yourself happy or your parents happy?"

"That's tough." He rubs his chin. "But it's not something I can answer for you. I think you gotta follow your heart on that one."

Well, that isn't very helpful.

"Thanks, Manuel," I say anyway.

After he leaves, I'm a giant pretzel of conflicting emotions.

What does it mean to follow my heart, anyway? What if pleasing my parents and wanting to do comedy are both pieces of my heart?

Unheard Voicemail from Mom

Yumi, did you get a lot of studies done at hagwon today? I hope so. Just a few more days before the big exam. Remember what we always say, you can do it! Also don't forget Daddy's speaker installation is today, so we have to close the restaurant. We were thinking maybe we can go visit your sister. She has day off from Starbucks, too. Maybe we can go to the Diddy Riese for the ice cream sandwich? You love that walnut one! We will pick you up from library early at one o'clock. See you! Don't forget to put on the sunscreen!

CHAPTER 19

I feel like a total fraud sitting here in the Haha Club lobby working on set design with my friends like everything is normal when really I'm heartbroken. In just a couple more hours, I'm going to walk out of camp for the final time without even saying goodbye. And no one knows except me.

But this is how it has to go.

Now that I see how Operation Show-My-Case was doomed to fail from the beginning, despite how much I wanted it to work out, it makes the most sense to cut my losses and leave it all behind. My friends, my idol, and my dreams of doing comedy. It sucks, but it's the easiest way to get out of this mess I've made for myself. Once I sneak my note and Yuri's check into Jasmine's purse, I can disappear like I was never here at all.

Well, it's a good thing that being invisible is one thing I'm pretty good at.

A heavy sigh escapes from me.

The sound of Felipe snapping his fingers in front of my face snatches me out of my whirlwind of thoughts.

"Hello, anybody home?"

"Sorry. Spaced out there, didn't I?" My cheeks are hot from shame.

"No worries." Felipe scribbles on the butcher paper. "I was just asking who you invited to come to tomorrow's showcase."

I pause, capping my marker. "Oh, I'm not sure yet."

Felipe and Sienna look at me as if they want me to elaborate.

I poke around the marker box for another color.

Felipe rolls his eyes. "My mom is so embarrassing. She went all out and invited the whole familia. Even my tío Rogelio, who lives way out in Pomona."

This guy. He has no idea how good he has it. What I'd do for my parents to support me like that. Shoot, I'd sign on to dishpit duty for a whole month if that meant Mom and Dad would come watch me perform.

"What about you, Sienna?" Felipe asks.

"My nanny is coming," she replies.

"What about your parents?" I ask.

"Nope." She doesn't look up.

"What? Are you serious?"

"Why not?" Felipe asks.

"Work."

"That sucks," Felipe says quietly.

"It is what it is." Then Sienna turns to me. "*People* think I'm so lucky to be Stanley and Jade Weston's kid, but they don't know about how lonely it is most of the time."

"I'm sorry, Sienna." I don't know what else to say.

"It's fine." She sniffs loudly.

"How are you feeling about it?" Felipe asks.

"Not awesome." She takes a deep breath. "I told them about the showcase weeks ago, and they promised they'd be there, but something always comes up with them. They gave me some excuse about how they didn't get the shot they needed, so they have to go back on location again this weekend."

I'm stunned.

"Whatever. I guess I should be used to it by now."

Sienna shakes the purple Sharpie, but it's out of ink. "I'll be right back."

When she gets up to find another purple marker, Felipe leans toward me. "Really sucks Sienna's parents aren't coming."

I nod. "Yeah."

"People aren't always who they seem." He scratches his chin and looks at me intently. "Did you get a chance to read the Beetleman comic book I lent you?"

I perk up, glad to switch the subject. "Yeah, I did."

"What'd you think?"

"It was so good. The ending smashed me in the guts, though."

"Right?"

"I can't believe Beetleman revealed his true identity in front of everyone. Isn't that, like, a big superhero no-no?"

"It was a good twist."

"Yeah, I totally didn't see that one coming. Thanks for letting me borrow it. I'll give it back . . . soon."

My mood plummets when I realize I will never be able to return it. In fact, I might not see him ever again after I leave here today.

"Keep it as long as you want." Felipe pauses. "So, uh. Speaking of secret identities. I want to ask you about something that's been on my mind."

"Sure. What is it?"

He fidgets with his shoelaces but then stops. "Listen, you know that I'm your friend, and you can trust me. Is there anything you want to tell me . . . about who you really are? Yumi?"

A sudden coldness hits me at my core.

He knows.

Fear paralyzes me. What am I supposed to tell him? I can't explain all this. Not here, not now. Besides, even if I did, he'd never understand.

I force out a quick bark of laughter. "I have no idea what you're talking about, Felipe." I grab the butcher paper and start rolling it up loudly.

He crosses his arms. "Whatever. Forget it."

I swallow hard, pretending not to notice.

In a week, he won't even remember I ever existed.

I'm actually relieved that the rest of camp is dress rehearsal for the showcase. All I have to do is sit in this dark auditorium until it's time to go. Two more hours. I can do this.

Reaching into my backpack, I take out the now-battered envelope containing my apology letter and payment and tuck it into my back pocket for easy access.

"Campers, please take your seats. This is our final run-through before tomorrow's big show!" Jasmine says before turning down the house lights.

I'm headed to the very back row so I don't have to deal with Felipe or Sienna, but before I'm even seated, my name is called from across the stage. "Kay?"

"Y-yes?"

"You're up first," Jasmine says.

Ugh, I forgot that I have to go onstage, too. It's bad enough I'm going to miss the showcase. Now I have to fake-rehearse for a show I won't even be at. Lovely.

I drag myself up the stairs.

The way the stage lights beat down on my shoulders reminds me of the first time I stood on this stage. That fateful day when everything changed. My first day of camp.

You lion cheetah.

That was the joke that got me my first laugh.

How ironic. Because that's exactly what I've become: a lying cheater.

I look out at the campers' faces in the audience. Then at Jasmine. This whole time I've been lying to them about who I am. Guilt wraps around my heart like a python squeezing its prey.

"Uh. Hi, everyone." I take a quick glance at my notebook, feeling nauseous.

At that moment, the back doors burst open, and a girl around my age comes rolling down the aisle in a wheelchair. Both her legs are propped up in casts.

What on earth?

A petite lady wearing a messy bun and yoga pants chases after her.

"Slow down, honey! Not so fast."

The girl points at Jasmine Jasper excitedly as she approaches us.

"There she is, Mom. It's her!" she whispers so loudly we can all hear.

I look around, and every camper has the same confused expression as me. What is up with this random girl barging into our rehearsal?

"Hello, can I help you with something?" Jasmine asks.

"Whoa, I'm so stoked to meet you in real life, Ms. Jasper," the girl says, with zero chill. "I've watched every single one of your YouTube videos, like, a million times. I'm your biggest fan."

"I'm sorry, but we're in the middle of camp right now. Is there something you need—"

The girl's mother jogs over to them. "My daughter is here for your camp. The doctor finally took her off bed rest today." She says it like Jasmine's supposed to know what she's talking about.

"I'm not sure I understand." Jasmine waits for an explanation. A bad feeling comes over me.

The mom digs around in her purse. "Oh, I explained our situation when I called the office last week. I spoke to one of your interns. Also, I sent an email. Didn't you get it?"

"No, I'm sorry, I didn't," Jasmine replies. "This is the first I'm hearing about this."

"That's strange." The mom pulls her phone from her purse and scrolls with one finger. "I emailed the Haha Club from work yesterday. You sure you didn't get anything from Kelly.Nakamura@emailme.com?"

Oh no.

"Wait a second." Jasmine pauses, and her eyes flicker to me. "Nakamura?"

This cannot be happening. Not right now.

"That's right. Kelly Nakamura, mother of Kay Nakamura," the mom confirms, still scrolling.

A collective gasp comes from everyone at the Haha Club as they start to connect the dots. Nineteen pairs of shocked eyeballs laser into me.

Jasmine looks like she's seen a ghost. "If she's Kay Nakamura, then who is . . ."

Her eyes meet mine, and it's like she can see all the secrets inside me, like I have no skin to hide them.

I've been caught.

Everyone is waiting for me to explain.

I need to get out of here.

"I'm . . . I . . . I have to go."

Instinctively, I take off running. I don't even know

where I'm going. I jet out of there as fast as my legs will take me. Away from the wall of eyes. Away from the whispers. Away from the pointing. Away from it all. I'm not supposed to be here anyhow.

I speed down the stairs. Through the room. Out the door. Out of the building. It doesn't matter where—anywhere but here.

Jasmine bolts after me.

"Wait! Come back!" she shouts, chasing after me. "Who are you?"

She's right on my tail.

My pupils burn as they adjust to the harsh afternoon sun, but I sprint ahead faster, dodging moving cars, tears streaming down my face, blurring my vision.

"Watch out! Careful!" she calls after me.

A car horn blares, and a tan minivan screeches to a halt a mere inch from crashing into my body, blocking my way.

Trapped. I look up, and I can't believe my eyes.

It's Mom and Dad.

CHAPTER 20

Mom leaps out of the car screaming, "Yumi!"

She grabs me by the arms as Dad slams the minivan into park.

"What happened?" She searches my face and body for injuries. "Why're you crying? You get hurt?"

I sob hysterically, overwhelmed that this is unraveling and I'm powerless to stop it.

Jasmine comes running right behind me. "Thank goodness, I thought you got hit!"

My parents eye her suspiciously.

"Who are you?" Dad yells, looking her up and down. "Why you chasing our daughter? Parking lot is very dangerous place."

Jasmine halts, suddenly out of sorts. "These are your parents?"

I nod.

"Yes, um. Where do I begin?" She takes a big breath. "My name is Jasmine Jasper, and, well . . ." Her voice drags for a second. "Sorry, but I'm a little confused myself."

It's then that the campers spill out of the building onto the sidewalk, surrounding us. Watching us. Whispering. Like I'm some kind of one-person freak show.

Jasmine begins again. "So it looks like there's been a bit of a mix-up with your daughter, well, we know her as Kay . . ."

"Hey, that's my name, too!" the real Kay interjects from her wheelchair.

"Her name is really Yumi Chung," Felipe shouts, with his arms crossed over his chest. "It's amazing the information you can find on Google."

"The plot thickens," Sienna says, glowering at me.

Mom's eyes bulge with recognition. "Those kids, you said they were your hagwon tutors! Explain this."

Jasmine, thinking Mom was talking to her, starts to explain. "So, Kay, I mean Yumi, well, she's been in my comedy camp—"

"Comedy camp?" Dad interrupts, jerking his head to face me. "Why are you going to comedy camp? EXPLAIN!"

Tears stream down my face as I tell it all in a jumbled heap of hard-to-follow facts—the mix-up with the names, my continued attendance at comedy camp, PAMS, everything.

"Yumi, why did you do this?" Mom's face wrinkles with hurt, the same way it did when Yuri told her she'd quit medical school.

"Is this true? You've been lying to us? To everybody?" Dad asks.

I nod, my tears dripping onto the hot asphalt like rain.

Dad's jaw tenses. "Ms. Jasper, I'm sorry our daughter brought so much trouble to you. We are so ashamed."

"I'm really sorry," I whisper to her. "I never meant for it to turn out like this."

I take out the envelope from my back pocket. "I was going to give you this today. It's a letter and the payment for camp."

Jasmine stares at the crinkled envelope before finally taking it. "I don't know what to say. I didn't expect this from you."

Hearing her say that destroys me. I let her down. I let everyone down. All because I was trying to be the New Me.

"Well, it looks like you have a lot to discuss with your family," Jasmine says. She turns to my parents. "Please, if you need anything from me, you can call me at the Haha Club."

She waves her hand at the gawking crowd. "All right, campers, let's get back inside. We have rehearsals to finish." She herds the curious, whispering kids back inside, leaving me alone with Mom and Dad.

We drive home in silence, my future completely up in the air.

CHAPTER 21

When we get home, Mom goes straight to the kitchen and clangs around like she always does when she's upset. Nabi whimpers but won't leave my side, sensing my unease.

I follow Dad to the living room like a lamb to slaughter, bracing myself for a scathing lecture with lots of yelling, but instead he collapses into his armchair and stares into the space in front of him with unfocused eyes. He grips his forehead with his palm and squeezes his eyes shut like he's got a severe migraine.

"So, this is why you haven't scored ninety-eighth percent yet. You have been wasting your time with comedy foolishness instead of studying like you were supposed to?"

I knew he'd say this, but his words still slice me inside.

"No, Dad, I've been studying. So much. I've done

everything Mrs. Pak told me to do. I'm actually really close—"

He shakes his head slowly, willfully ignoring my voice.

"Your Mom and I sacrifice so much. We're working like dogs at the restaurant for you and your sister to have better life."

I don't have enough courage to lift my eyes when his voice quavers.

"And this is how you repay? So ungrateful!"

He turns his back to me.

"Go to your room. I have no more to say."

I scoop up Nabi and climb the stairs with tears falling steadily down my cheeks. He's so wrong about me. I'm not the unappreciative daughter that he thinks I am. I do appreciate how hard they work. How can I not? *I'm* tired, and I only do half of what they do. Every time I go to the restaurant, I see how tough it is for them. And every cent they make has gone toward our education—Yuri's medical school, Winston, hagwon.

But just because I want to do comedy doesn't make me selfish. Mom and Dad don't understand that the stage is my lifeboat. The one place where I'm able to let go and make mistakes and figure it out as I go without penalty. I wish I could make them see how much it frees me.

But I can't. I'm not allowed.

I do as I'm told and go to my room, jam-packed with things I don't have the courage to say out loud.

Like I always do, I reach for my Super-Secret Comedy Notebook, but when I open it up, it brings me nothing but sadness. The thoughts, observations, and secrets that I've been recording are what got me into this mess, and there's nothing funny about that.

Bitter, I fling it across my room as hard as I can, and it crashes against the back of my closet wall, sending Nabi fleeing under the bed.

I pull out my phone to text Sienna and Felipe. I want to explain everything, but I don't know quite where to begin. After a few attempts, I simply type "I'm so sorry."

Send.

I wait and wait for who knows how long, but the three gray dots in the reply box never appear.

They're ignoring me.

I guess I can't really blame them. After all, I did assume a fake identity, build a friendship on deceit, and point-blank lie to Felipe's face when he asked for the truth. Even I wouldn't want to be friends with someone like me.

I dial Yuri, but it goes straight to voicemail.

Surprise, surprise.

Lately, she's hardest to track down when I need her most. It's just as well, I suppose. Pretty soon she'll be halfway around the world doing stuff that's way more important than me. She won't be able to pick up the phone and help me with my petty problems then. Might as well get used to it now.

The rest of the night, I lie awake in bed, listening to the sounds of my parents arguing downstairs, blaming each other for raising a disappointment like me. I blink away the tears, feeling numb as everything crashes down.

The restaurant is in trouble. Yuri is moving away. Felipe and Sienna will probably never talk to me again. Jasmine thinks I'm a liar. My parents think I'm the most rotten daughter on the planet. And I might as well kiss my hopes of going to PAMS goodbye.

And worst of all, I'm right back to who I was before.

The Old Me.

CHAPTER 22

Yuri and I are unloading her stuff from the U-Haul to store in the garage while she's away in Nepal. But my mind is somewhere else. All I can think about is how the camp showcase happened today and I have no idea how it went.

"Who knew I had so much stuff?" Yuri drags a crate across the ground with all her might. "I can't believe I'm going to be living out of a backpack for the next two years."

"Yup." I focus on stacking the boxes along the back wall, not much in the mood for conversation.

She unfolds a lawn chair. "How about we stop for a break?"

"Great, I'm pooped," I grumble, planting myself on a big box. I reach for my phone only to remember, oh yeah, my parents confiscated it this morning.

"Can I borrow your phone again?"

"Sure." She tosses it to me, and I immediately scroll through the Haha Club's social media to see if anyone has posted anything from the showcase.

I refresh a bunch of times. "Still nothing."

"You sure you want to keep checking? Isn't that going to make you feel worse?"

"Probably."

Even though I'm "forbidden to affiliate" with the Haha Club people for the rest of my natural life, that doesn't mean I'm not dying to know what's going on with them. The FOMO is strong—I have to lurk; there's too much I want to know. Was it a packed house? Did Sienna do her joke about the cow doing yoga? Did Felipe end up wearing his red velvet or rainbow sequin bow tie?

Yuri frowns as I hand her back her phone. "What are you going to do without my phone when I leave for Nepal?"

My face falls. "Don't remind me."

I tug at my shirt. The real question is, what am I going to do without my big sister?

I let out a long sigh.

"I'll return before you know it." She tousles my hair, but suddenly jumps back, letting out a bloodcurdling scream.

"What? What is it?" I yelp.

She points wildly at the top of my head, horrified. Yuri covers her mouth with both hands. "Spider!"

I thrash and scream. My whole body flares up, and suddenly there are creepy crawly sensations all over my body. I swear I feel tarantula hairs skittering across the nape of my neck. I bend over, violently flinging my head and raking my fingers through my hair, trying to shake out what I'm convinced is an entire black widow colony.

"Stop! Don't move," Yuri screams. She tiptoes over to me like a spy. "Shh." She grabs a curling iron from a box and grips it like a baseball bat. "Hold. Still. I've got a good angle."

"Do you see any bite marks?"

I'm feeling woozy. This is what it's like to have black widow venom in my system. How much time do I have before my major organs shut down?

"Hold still!" Yuri instructs me.

I crouch into the fetal position, my life flashing before my eyes. So many dreams unfulfilled. I've never even been to a BTS concert.

There's a whoosh of air dangerously close to my scalp, and a scraggly black thing goes sailing through the air and lands on the concrete floor.

"You got it?"

"I think so." Yuri stomps on it with her sneaker, but when she lifts her foot, she bursts into laughter.

I bend to take a closer look.

What the heck?

"Seriously, Yuri?" I pick it up. It's a tangled ball of black thread. "You almost gave me a heart attack."

"Sorry, it looked just like a spider . . ." A deep laugh erupts from her. "You should have seen your face, though."

"Very funny."

She bulges her eyes in mock terror, which makes me crack a smile.

She does it again, and I can't resist laughing.

It reminds me of a joke.

"Hey, why should you never trust a spider?"

Yuri shakes her head. "I don't know. Why?"

"Because they always post stuff on the web," I say with a straight face.

We cackle together some more until our sides hurt.

"Aw, Yooms. You must be feeling better if you're making jokes again." She bops me with her elbow.

Then she gives me a curious sideways glance. "Have you talked to Mom and Dad?"

"Just a little this morning." I sink back on the box.

"How are things going?"

I cross my arms. "About what you'd expect." Which means we're pretending nothing happened, but obviously something did because the screen door's hinges are busted from all the slamming.

"How are things at the restaurant?"

I shrug. "Mom told me to take some time off from helping out to concentrate on studying for my test."

"That's serious. She never does that."

"Yeah, I'm actually relieved. It'll be nice to get a break

from all their bickering. That's all they do these days."

"They have a lot on their minds, Yumi."

"You're telling me. They're so consumed with the Grand Reopening, they don't even care about me and my problems right now."

"No, they do. They're stressed. That's all."

Whatever. I'll always be invisible to them.

I stretch my legs and yawn. I don't want to talk about this anymore. "Yuri, you know you can't freak out every time you think you see a spider."

I bend to pick up the scraggle of black thread from the ground. "There's probably going to be a bunch of spiders at the farms you're staying at."

"Oh no, you're probably right." She nods like she's realizing it for the first time. "I need to make sure to bring enough bug spray."

She gets up and takes out two banana milk boxes from the extra fridge in the garage. She tosses one to me and takes a long sip of hers.

"I got my first assignment. We're going to be teaching gardening techniques."

I stifle a giggle. "Yuri, what do you know about gardening?" I don't think I've ever seen my sister touch dirt in my whole life. She's, like, the biggest clean-freak germophobe ever.

"I guess I'll have to learn on the job." She plays with her straw. "It'll be an adventure. That's what I've been wanting, right?"

She lets out a nervous chuckle like she's trying to convince me or herself or both.

I chug my banana milk.

"Don't worry," I say. "You're going to have the best time."

She'll get to journey from one village to the next, learning new things with her new, interesting friends, free from Mom and Dad's rules and expectations. I'm getting jealous just thinking about it. Except not the spider part.

"Think about how great it'll be to do whatever you want for a change."

"That's true." Yuri smiles weakly and then checks the time. "I've got to return this moving van before they close." She pulls the keys from her pocket. "I have an idea. On the way back, we can get some patbingsu."

"No, thanks." I brush off the dust from my shorts. For once, the allure of shaved ice has no hold on me.

"C'mon, I'll buy you the giant matcha green tea one you like," she says with a wink. "With mochi balls?"

I finish the banana milk and toss it into the trash can. "You go. I'm going to take Nabi for a walk."

Maybe that'll help me forget the fact my sister is leaving me and I'm missing the camp showcase.

Nabi wags her fluffy little tail as I leash her up. The summer sun is finally starting to set, and the heat is subsiding. I'm not much of a runner, but that's just about the only thing my parents will let me do outside the house unsupervised.

I head out to go around the block. My feet hit the pavement in a steady rhythm, and slowly I pick up the pace. The dry Santa Ana wind gusts through my hair as I try to empty my brain, but thoughts keep sweeping their way in.

I wonder what Jasmine thinks of me now. Did she ever read the letter I wrote her?

I pump my legs faster and faster.

Who am I kidding? She probably thinks I'm no different from that shady student of hers, the one who stole her notebook. My heart pounds in my chest. She hates me, I know it. I can practically feel it.

My heart rate speeds as I jog down the block. The streetlamps that line the sidewalks flicker on, and the sky is a pink-lemonade-and-whipped-cream swirl. I remember my old science teacher once explained that our colorful sunsets are due, in part, to all the pollution in the air. Who knew how beautiful smog could be under the right conditions?

Nabi is panting hard, and her pace slows.

"C'mon, girl, you can't stop now. We've got to hurry if we want to get back home before dark." Or else my parents will probably panic and call 911 to file a missing person report.

She makes a whining sound and defiantly plants her butt down, letting me know she's had enough exercise for the day.

"All right, you win." Lazy little dog.

I tug on her leash, signaling we'll be walking the rest of the way.

We turn onto the main road to take the fastest route home, past familiar parking lots and shopping plazas.

Nabi stops to do her business right in front of the Comic Underworld store. While I wait for her to finish, I can't resist taking a peek through the store window.

My heart aches.

There in the back, I can make out the issues of Beetle-man, Chameleon Girl, and Ninja Girl still sitting on the shelf where we left them a few days ago. When things were so different.

Suddenly, I'm flooded with memories and I'm an emotional mess. I remember the time Felipe and I cho-reographed our robot dance routine. And the time Sienna gave me a pair of socks she tie-dyed in my favor-ite colors.

They were such good friends to me.

Now every time I pass this place I'll be reminded of how I ruined everything.

My side cramps.

It's getting dark, so I bag up Nabi's poop and head for home.

CHAPTER 23

Mrs. Pak's timer chimes, indicating the end of class. It's hard to believe I made it to the final hagwon session of the summer.

As we're getting our things, Mrs. Pak raps her pointer on the whiteboard like a woodpecker.

"Attention, students. A few announcements," she says, quieting us.

Clack. Clack. Clack. Clack. The sharp sounds of her footsteps still make my blood pressure climb.

Mrs. Pak takes off her glasses. "As you know, today concludes our Test Prep 101 class. You've all grown so much during our time together. I've pushed you, and you've studied diligently, and I hope that you'll continue to pursue excellence beyond these walls. I expect to hear lots of good news soon."

To my surprise, someone starts clapping, and we all join in.

"All right. That's enough."

Mrs. Pak, who I didn't think was capable of blushing, lifts one hand for silence.

"Thank you for all your hard work this summer, students. Good luck in your future academic endeavors."

On the way out, she smiles warmly at me.

"Great effort, Yumi. I'm very proud of your progress. I have a feeling I'll be adding you to my Wall of Excellence in a few years if you keep it up."

I beam, not knowing quite how to respond. "Thank you . . . for everything."

That Mrs. Pak. She's an acquired taste for sure, but I think I might actually miss her.

Outside in the hallway, Ginny holds up her hand for a high five.

"Woo-hoo! I never thought this day would come," she says with a grin across her face. "We're finally free."

She spins around in circles with her arms outstretched.

"For now, I guess." Until Winston starts up in just a

few short weeks. I sling on my backpack with a sigh.

"Still bummed about not going to PAMS?" Ginny asks.

"Yeah." A lump forms in my throat.

"I'm sorry about what happened." Ginny nods sympathetically. "It really stinks."

"It's fine. I'll get used to it." I don't want to ruin the good feels. "Since it's the last day, do you want to celebrate with a taco truck run?"

Ginny says, "No, I'm good. My mom packed this yummy bulgogi for me."

I do a double take. "You're eating beef now?" I take a seat at the lunch table. "What happened to *feed it, don't eat it?*"

She gets out her bento box from her backpack. "I'm still vegan." She pops off the lid to show me. "Check it out. My mom made bulgogi out of soy curls."

"Soy curls?" That sounds like a bad hairstyle my mom would try to force on me.

"They're dehydrated strips of soy protein made out of whole, non-GMO soybeans. They're a great meat alternative."

She stashes the container in the ancient wood-paneled microwave and punches a few buttons.

"So tell me, I'm dying to know: how'd you ever get your mom to finally support your veganism?" I take out a bag of Hot Cheetos from my own backpack.

"Well, it was pretty simple. Instead of fighting, we just talked about it. I sat her down at the kitchen table and told her I was serious about making this lifestyle choice. At first, she blew me off like usual, but when I got out all the recipes and articles I'd printed, she saw how much it mattered to me."

"That's it?"

"Yup."

"Interesting." I nibble on my Hot Cheetos in disbelief. All summer long, Ginny's been fighting so hard for her mom to listen to her, and all she needed to do was explain in words why it meant so much.

The microwave beeps, and Ginny pulls out the steaming hot dish and sets it on the table.

I take a whiff. It sure looks and smells like beef. She hands me a forkful of the fake bulgogi. "Try it."

"Sure," I say, though I'd rather not. I don't want to be

rude, so I take a bite. Not bad. Not great. The flavor is right, but the consistency is more like Laffy Taffy than Korean-style thin-sliced marinated beef.

Hmm.

I can't believe I'm eating tofu curls.

More than that, I can't believe Ginny convinced her mom to cook vegan.

I guess nothing is impossible.

CHAPTER 24

If I spend another minute studying for the SSAT, my brain just might pop like an overinflated balloon. There's absolutely no space in there for any new information. With the test in two days, it's doubtful any last-minute cramming will make a huge difference anyway.

I need to take a break, and the savory aroma of dumplings sizzling in sesame oil wafting in from the kitchen is calling my name.

"Did you eat?" Mom asks, piling a dozen steaming dumplings onto a plate for me.

"Not yet." I grab a set of chopsticks.

Things must be thawing between my mom and me if she's actually cooking again. It's a good thing because, as much as I love Cinnamon Toast Crunch, I don't think I can stomach another bowl of cereal.

"Eat a lot." She sets down a tiny bowl of dipping sauce. "Cannot study on empty stomach."

Ah, out comes the real reason she's laying off me.

"How are things at the restaurant?"

"Very busy but almost ready for tomorrow," she says, flipping more dumplings in the frying pan. "Don't worry about it. We will take care of everything at Grand Reopening. Just come. You focus on getting the scholarship." Mom takes off her apron and points back upstairs. "After you eat, I want you to clean your room. Cannot concentrate on your work in that mess!"

"Okay." I relent, doing what I can to placate her.

After I polish off my dumplings, I trudge back to my room to survey the damage.

Eesh. It's been so hectic these days, I haven't noticed that my room has slowly devolved into a hazardous waste zone unfit for human habitation.

Where to even begin?

I go with the biggest challenge first: my closet.

When I slide the door open, a huge mountain of stuff tumbles out, swallowing up the entire middle of my room.

Yuck. I start pitching things into the garbage. Empty bags of Hot Cheetos, old issues of *Girls' World*, stacks of Pokémon cards. All kinds of random stuff.

I comb through the debris and discover some long-forgotten Halloween candy in an old pillowcase. What's the expiration date on chocolate, anyway? Is ten months too old? Cautiously, I nibble on a Reese's Peanut Butter Cup. It's a little chalky, but surprisingly decent.

I'm making progress thinning the heap of junk when, from the corner of my eye, I spy my Super-Secret Comedy Notebook poking out from the pile.

I jump to retrieve it.

It's only been a couple of days since I threw it across my room in anger, but holding it again feels like I'm reconciling with an old friend.

I flip through and stop when I come upon the routine I'd planned to perform at the showcase. I laugh out loud as I reread it, but it'd be funnier if I changed the wording a bit.

I grab a pen to start making some tweaks, but then there's a knock at the door.

I stash my notebook and pen back under the pile.

"How's it going?" Mom asks, edging around the mound of miscellany. This is the first time she's set foot in my room since I got in trouble, which is part of the reason why it's in its current state.

"Pretty well."

"Yumi, you have so much junks in here." She riffles through my things carefully, like she's afraid she's going to catch the bubonic plague.

I inch to block her from where my notebook is hiding. "Sorry." One glance at it, and I'll be back to eating cereal for another week.

She reaches past me and picks up a sparkly rainbow sequin hair bow from the floor. She tries to keep a straight face. "Remember this?"

If only I could forget. Unfortunately, it's seared into my memory for life as one of my top embarrassing moments, and that's saying a lot. I wore that rainbow sequin bow and matching dress for my fifth-grade piano recital. Well, that is, before I got so nervous I barfed all over the stage. Good times.

She comes over to me and smooths my locks with her

hands, sweeping them to the side before she fastens the bow to the top of my head. It's a silly, babyish bow, and I wouldn't be caught dead wearing it outside, but I let her put it on because I kind of miss her doing my hair like she used to.

"You look so cute." She turns me to face the mirror. "Like when you were little."

"Mom, I look like a Christmas present." I laugh.

She combs her fingers through my limp strands, but then her face pinches. "Your hair is already losing the curl. Did you use the product I gave you?"

Her hair comment hits the wrong chord, and suddenly I'm all riled up.

"No."

"You should use it. Will make perm last longer."

I flinch. What's with her obsession with my appearance?

"I will call salon. Make appointment for you to get touch-up before school starts. I have to get my hair done, too. So busy with the restaurant, not enough time to take care of myself."

I swear, some things will never change. My parents

won't let me make my own choices, not even choices about my own hair.

"You okay, Yumi?" Mom spies the candy wrappers on my bed. "You should not eat this candy. Give you stomachache." She palms my forehead to take my temperature.

Suddenly, I'm like a kettle bubbling over with so many unsaid things.

"Mom, I don't want my hair permed anymore," I blurt out.

"What? Why? You need the volume." She cups the bottom of my hair and scrunches it up.

I sniff, tucking my legs under me.

"No, I'm tired of the kids at Winston calling me Top Ramen," I tell her with a catch in my voice.

I pick at the carpet, trying to keep my tears from falling.

Mom sits next to me and tucks my hair behind my ear. "That's a compliment. Means they think you are on top." She lifts her pointer finger. "The best! Number one!"

I roll my eyes. "No, Mom. That's not what they mean."

At Winston, I'm the opposite of number one. If

anything, I'm a negative one. With an absolute value of zero to the infinity power.

"They're making fun of me." Like when they imitate me when I get called on or when they take bets on how many words I'll say on a given day. "They also call me Yu-meat," I add, wiping the sides of my eyes.

"What is that? Why do they call you that?"

"Yu-MEAT. Because my clothes smell like barbecue. From the restaurant."

She narrows her eyes. "Next time, you can tell them that Chung's is best barbecue restaurant in Koreatown. Even have the karaoke. Bring your friends."

"This is not a joke."

"Focus on your studies. Don't pay attention to foolish kids." She rubs my back in circles with one hand like she used to when I got sick.

"Easy for you to say. You don't have to sit next to annoying Tommy Molina in homeroom."

"He has no manners, and his hair is too long," she huffs, balling the candy wrappers and tossing them into the trash bag. "Why you never told me the kids are mean to you at school?"

"I don't know. There's a lot of things I don't tell you."

Sadness wells in her eyes. "Yumi, it's not good to keep all the thoughts inside. You have to speak if you want people to hear you."

There's a weird awkward silence.

"I do speak up . . . in my comedy."

Mom's face hardens. "We already talked about that."

Well, technically we haven't. They never actually asked me *why* I did what I did. My parents still have no idea what comedy means to me. They just shut me down and doled out my punishment for disobeying them.

Mom gets up and dusts off her pants. "I have to go help your dad. I want this room clean when I get home."

"Sure."

And she wonders why I never open up to her.

CHAPTER 25

At long last, the big day my family has been waiting for is finally here: the restaurant's Grand Reopening.

The moment I step inside, the place is alive with activity. All the employees are scurrying around, pushing in chairs and wiping down tables.

"Is this really our restaurant?" Yuri whispers.

How did it transform so much in the week that I've been away?

The décor has been updated, from the wall color, to the layout of the tables, to the rice paper screen panels from the garage tastefully repurposed as wall hangings.

"What's wrong? Don't you like it?" my sister asks.

"I do, it's just . . . so different," I reply, noticing the luminous paper lanterns that now hang over the dining area. It looks way better, but part of me is sad that all the stuff I grew up with is now suddenly gone. But I remind myself that it's for the future. It's for the best. We'll make new memories here.

Mom comes in from down the hall wearing her gorgeous plum-and-emerald satin hanbok.

"Wow, Mom, you're stunning!" Yuri squeals.

Mom pats her updo with one hand to show off her jade ring, clearly enjoying all the fuss.

"How about restaurant?" she says with a twinkle in her eye. "What do you think?"

"Mom, it honestly could have come out of a catalog," my sister exclaims. "Did you decorate this by yourself?"

Mom smiles. "Why are you surprised? You know I have excellent taste."

She does. I'll give her that.

"Very impressive." I give her a side hug. While things between us have been rocky, on a day like today I'm willing to put all that stuff to the side so I can focus on what matters most: saving our restaurant.

"Hey, if it isn't the Chung sisters! Haven't seen you girls in a minute." Manuel enters the dining room. "My brother got it looking pretty classy in here, right?"

"Oscar hooked it up!" I high-five him.

"Cabal!" Manuel says.

"He did good job." Mom gestures to the floor. "Look at this! So clean and shiny now."

He grins. "Which reminds me, I got a good one for you."

"What?" I ask.

"Why is buffing the floors better than vacuuming?"

"I don't know. Why?"

"Because vacuums just suck."

Manuel is still laughing at his own joke when Dad comes rushing in from the kitchen dressed in a three-piece suit with his hair gelled to the side.

"Check out this guy! Is that you, Bong? Or is it James Bong?" Manuel says.

"I like that. James Bong. Very funny!" Dad holds his gun-fingers 007 style and laughs. He turns to Manuel. "You think it's better button or no button?"

Manuel dusts the tops of Dad's shoulders with both hands. "It's sharp unbuttoned. You look good. Don't be nervous. It'll be fine."

"I hope so." Dad exhales deeply and then checks the clock. "It's almost time."

He calls us and all the employees to gather around him for a meeting. "In just few minutes, we will open and have a new beginning at Chung's Barbecue. Thank you for all your hard work to prepare for today. Let's give best service to our guests," he says with the gusto of a game show host.

He urges us to put our hands together into a pile like we're on a Little League team and yells, "Fighting!"—the Korean version of "Let's do this!"

The pep rally breaks up, and Mom approaches us with a shopping bag in hand.

"Hurry. Go change into this."

I take a peek. "Seriously, Mom?"

One look at her face, and it's clear. Yes, she is very serious.

Reluctantly, we change into the matching pink-and-yellow silk hanboks we usually wear only for New Year's celebrations and family portraits.

"It's so itchy and stiff, even with my shorts and T-shirt underneath." I fuss with the empire waistline.

"You look like a Korean princess. Here, let me help you with that." Yuri straightens my sloppy sash, then pulls my stray hairs back into my low-slung bun.

"Do you really think this is going to work? Can we really earn back all that money we owe Mr. Montgomery in just one night?" I ask, smoothing out my skirt.

"I hope so. We have no choice, right?" She pins my gold name badge to my top.

When it's five o'clock, we take our station at the hostess stand, and Dad flips the sign to OPEN.

"Here goes nothing," Yuri whispers to no one in particular.

My heart pounds, and I cross my fingers for good luck.

It must have worked, because just a little bit later, the air is smoky with the tantalizing smell of grilled meat, and we're busy serving the tables and tables of guests. I can't remember the last time our place was this crowded. It's been months, maybe years!

Yuri and I struggle to keep pace getting people in and out the door. We set tables, bring menus, and seat guests at warp speed. Mom runs around taking orders and ringing up tickets. It's ridiculously chaotic, but I don't care; as long as we're on our way to paying Mr.

Montgomery back and keeping our restaurant, I'm all about it.

Dad zooms by, smiling from ear to ear.

"See, you girls need to trust your daddy. I told you this is going to be a big success."

He floats around greeting the guests with that extra level of service. He's so into it, Mom has to scold him for giving out too many orders of her famous mandu dumplings on the house.

Relief washes over me. "I have to hand it to Dad. At this rate, we are going to end up with a surplus."

"I'm not sure about that, but it's certainly going better than I expected," Yuri says.

I poke her in the arm. "But have you noticed that not one person has used the karaoke machine? We spent so much money building that stage . . ."

She shushes me. "Don't jinx it with negativity. Anyway, food and drink sales generate revenue, not karaoke."

"True."

We should be glad people are here at all. Singing or not.

As the night wears on, however, the energy slows,

and by seven, the steady stream of customers comes to an abrupt stop, like someone shut off the faucet.

"What happened?" I ask Yuri, poking my head outside.

No one is there.

"It's supposed to be prime time for dinner rush."

Mom paces nervously before coming over to our station.

"Any new guests?"

We shake our heads.

She punches in numbers on the cash register keyboard with this look on her face like she's given in and can't wait any longer.

"Why are you checking that now, Mom?" I ask. Usually she goes over the stats on the day's inventory after closing.

"Ka man isseo," she shushes, scrolling through the spreadsheets.

I hate it when she disregards me.

"Wait. That can't be." Yuri hovers over her shoulder, calculating the numbers in her head. "The dining room has been full for two solid hours. How is that all the money we've made?"

My mom turns the key and opens the register tray. She hands us the giant stack of coupons. It reads 50% OFF YOUR DINNER FROM 5:00 PM TO 7:00 PM FOR OUR GRAND REOPENING.

"Are you telling me that's why everyone was here earlier? Because of these coupons?" I ask, handing them back to her.

"Yes, it's great bargain for them," Mom explains in a lowered voice. "Not for us."

"So even though we fed all those people, we only made half the money?" I scratch my head, still trying to figure out the math. "Isn't that . . . bad?"

Yuri crosses her arms. "If you factor in the cost of the food and the staff wages, we're losing money with this promotion."

"This your father's great idea." Mom glances toward Dad, who is on the stage adjusting the sound on the karaoke equipment no one has bothered to use. It's then I notice the dark circles under his eyes and the worry on his face.

"The only way we can hit our target profit is if each table tips twenty percent, orders drinks and appetizers, and we keep our restaurant at full capacity for the rest of the night," Yuri says solemnly.

Nerves set in as we look around the nearly empty restaurant.

We don't say anything more because there's nothing we can do but hope and wait.

So we wait, and it's painfully slow. Like watching soybean paste ferment.

Dad comes by again.

"Don't worry." He laughs, putting on a brave face. "They will come. It's weekend. People like to eat late these days."

I want to believe him. I *really* want to believe him, but everything around me tells me he's dead wrong about this.

Over the next hour, only two families come in.

I check and recheck the register, telling myself there's still time. Maybe if a few waves of big groups eat here one after another and they tip generously, we might still be able to make it. But as minutes tick into hours and nothing happens, our hope starts to shrivel up.

Dad stops dropping by to give us pep talks.

By eight o'clock, panic sets in and even Dad cannot mask his distress. With only one last hour remaining, we need a Disney-sized miracle.

In an act of sheer desperation, Dad goes outside and invites the people passing by to come in.

"Grand Reopening. Come eat Korean barbecue and sing the karaoke!"

Unsurprisingly, no one takes him up on it. Dad, with disheveled hair and fraught bloodshot eyes, isn't exactly the picture of welcoming hospitality he was earlier.

A full half hour before the official closing time, Dad comes to grips with reality and calls the employees together for a meeting in the back room.

"Thank you for working so hard today. Business is slow. You can go home early. We will take care of the cleanup tonight."

It's awkward, but I think it's clear what's going on. We didn't get enough people in the door, and he's cutting his losses with their hourly wages.

Nervous glances are exchanged as the servers get their things to go.

Dad glances at Manuel. "Mrs. Chung can handle cooking for the rest of night. You can go, too."

"You got it." On his way out, Manuel whispers to my dad, "It's not over until it's over, Bong."

By nine o'clock, nothing's happened and it's over for real.

Dad flips the sign to CLOSED, shuts off the audio equipment onstage, and heads to the kitchen by himself.

We clean with silent tears in our eyes.

CHAPTER 26

"Check the balance," Mom instructs Yuri.

My sister clicks through the multiple screens on the office computer. "Well, including the money Uncle from San Jose sent plus the money we made tonight, we are still short about six thousand dollars."

"Aigoo. Six thousand dollars . . ." Mom repeats, not even trying to hide the hopelessness in her voice.

"Now what? What are we going to do?" I ask frantically.

A disconcerting unease comes over me seeing the adults who are supposed to be in charge look as confused as me.

"Maybe it's time we stop doing the restaurant," Mom finally answers.

It's like a slap in the face.

"What do you mean, *stop doing the restaurant*?" I ask. "Are you suggesting that we give up?"

Mom sits on the chair. "San Jose Uncle wants to buy another dry-cleaning business. A few months ago, he asked Daddy to move to San Jose to help him. Be manager. He says it's easier than restaurant business."

"Mom, no. We can't move to San Jose!"

"Calm down, Yooms," Yuri says. "We have to go over all our options and evaluate what's best for our family right now."

Am I the only one who cares about saving our restaurant? Hello, I took my first steps clutching onto the chairs right here in this very dining room. We celebrated every birthday with dduk made in this kitchen. I did my homework in that booth. Helped pack takeout orders and refill soy sauce bottles before I could read. Most of my bits and jokes were written on the office couch. All here. And let's not get started on our staff. I have known Manuel and his family my whole life. They're the ones who introduced me to DJ Keoki and sweet quesadillas! What about them? And Mom is talking about throwing in the towel? Now?

"How can you say that? It's not over yet. Los Angeles is our home. Chung's Barbecue is our home. We need to figure out a way to stay. We still have two days to make that money back!"

Again no one responds to me. Can they even hear me?

"Yumi, can you take out trash to dumpster?" Mom finally says.

It's clear from her tone that she's exhausted and wants me out of the room so she can talk to Yuri about "grown-up" things without having to deal with my childish hysteria.

"Fine." I could use some fresh air, anyway.

I chuck the drippy black garbage sacks from the kitchen onto the cart.

Frustrated, I kick the back door open and shove the heavy cart with all my might through the doorway.

But then I smell something in the air.

Who's smoking out here?

Off in the distance, I see Dad sitting on an overturned crate with his back to me, holding a cigarette between his fingers.

My stomach sinks. He only smokes when he's really stressed out.

Then I notice his body shaking. What could be so funny at a time like this? Has he completely lost it?

And then I realize he's not laughing—he's weeping.

I gasp. I've never seen my dad cry in my whole life.

He takes a puff from his cigarette like he's trying to stop his cries from escaping, but they do anyway.

It destroys me.

Before he notices, I duck back inside, but I accidentally bump the cart, sending all the bags crashing to the ground.

Startled, Dad turns around, and our eyes meet.

Oh no.

He flings his cigarette and stomps on it to put it out. He wipes his face with his sleeves.

"S-sorry, I can do this later," I say, pushing the door back open.

To my surprise, he waves me over. "Yumi, come here."

Uncertain, I make my way to him, averting my gaze to give him privacy.

I pull another crate next to him.

Neither of us speak.

When I wrap my arms around myself to protect

against the brisk night air, Dad takes off his jacket and puts it on my shoulders.

Then, after what feels like an eternity, he says, "I'm sorry."

"For what?" I whisper, fighting back my own tears.

He lets out a deep breath. "Karaoke stage was terrible idea."

It unsettles me to hear him talk like this. Dad's the guy who makes something from nothing and doesn't apologize to anyone. The guy who makes me feel safe and secure. Why is he apologizing to me?

I search for the right words that might restore his confidence. "No, Dad. What are you talking about? It's not your fault. Not at all. It was only one slow day, that's all."

He blinks his glassy eyes several times. "I thought I was smart to do the original idea, but maybe there is a reason no restaurant has karaoke stage in Koreatown."

"Maybe people just haven't heard about it yet. Maybe tomorrow there'll be more people," I offer, desperately trying to reassure him. "We still have time, Dad. We still have until Monday."

Dad shakes his head. "No, not enough time. We do

not have enough time," he says quietly. "It's done."

His words leave me hollow. I want to tell him he's wrong. I want him to come to his senses and be Dad again, but the defeat on his face tells me he's serious. He is finished.

"Now you understand why I want you to study hard?"

"Study?"

"If you become lawyer or doctor, you will make a lot of money." He motions to the restaurant behind us. "You will not have to worry about this money stress."

He's told me this a million times before, but today it feels different. It doesn't feel like just something parents say to nag their kids. It feels raw and true. Like he means it from his bones.

"I am immigrant. I have no choice to do this hard work. But you." He touches my cheek. "You can work in an office or hospital and be great success one day. You will work with your mind, not your hands."

He looks down.

"I'm sorry I did not provide with this restaurant, but we will keep working and find new jobs so you can have everything you need to go to college."

My heart swells and aches at the same time. Even after he poured fifteen years of his blood, sweat, and tears into Chung's Barbecue and it's about to be taken from him, the only thing he's concerned about is my future.

"Are we going to move to San Jose so you can work for Uncle?"

Dad recoils, the light returning to his eyes. "No, I told your mom a hundred times we will never do that." His voice is indignant. "I will rather scrub the toilet and work five jobs."

Okay, he's back. *This* is the Dad I know.

Then he adds, "We must stay here so you can go to Winston."

"Dad—"

"I know you want to go to the other school, but Winston will give you better chance to get into good university. You need the best education. I cannot let you suffer like me."

I look up at the twinkling buildings scattered across the downtown skyline, desperately wishing that Dad could understand what comedy means to me.

Then it occurs to me that this is my chance to tell him.

After all, that's all it took for Ginny's mom to come around.

"Dad?" I shift, mustering my courage. "I . . . really love comedy," I blurt out.

There's an uncertain moment of silence.

I try again. "What I mean is, it's everything to me. When I'm onstage, people actually listen to me. And when I get people to laugh, it's the best. It makes me feel like a whole different person, and I don't want to stop. That's why I did what I did."

When Dad starts laughing softly to himself, I don't know how to react.

"Daddy understands you."

My neck swings. "You do?"

Not to be mean, but Dad's pretty much the most unfunny person in the existence of humankind. He doesn't even get the punch lines of jokes on commercials.

"I will tell you my secret." He stops, like he's not quite sure if he should or not.

I lean in close. "What?"

"When I was young, I wanted to be a gasu."

He nudges me with his shoulder.

"You? A singer?" I think about it. "You know, that makes a lot of sense."

He's got a great voice, and he's pretty comfortable on the stage. Too comfortable. He could live up there, honestly.

There's a confessional glint in his eye. "When I was a young man, I wanted to be famous singer." He laughs out loud. "I was best singer in my school. So popular. Best in my town. I wanted to be the next Elton John. Pop rock star. Cool hair and big sunglasses. That was my dream." He closes his eyes for a moment as if he's playing his best highlights reel behind his eyelids.

"So, what happened?" I ask, suddenly curious about this mysterious side of Dad I never knew.

"I came to America, and I realize I cannot support my family as a gasu. So I bought this restaurant." He rests his hand on my shoulder. "You see, sometimes we have to do the practical thing, not the dream thing."

I nod. Hearing about the dreams Dad has let go for us sits in my stomach like a sack of sand.

"Being on the stage is such great feeling. I agree," Dad says with a smile.

"And the applause at the end, right?"

"Yes, best sound."

He puts his arm around me and hugs me tight. "No matter what, I want you to know that your mommy and daddy want to give you good things, very best things. Education is great gift, especially in America. Maybe you don't understand yet, but we are happy to sacrifice for your future. You know that?"

I nod.

"You know your mom sold her diamond earrings to pay for your hagwon tuition?"

"What? She did?" I'm saddled with guilt. "Those were her favorite . . . "

"I tell you so you will understand how much she wants best for you. She will give up her best things so you can have best things. Please trust and obey your parents, okay? Talking together is better than sneaky lies."

"Yes, Dad."

I exhale.

While I wasn't able to convince him to send me to PAMS, my heart is full knowing that he actually listened to me. I've never felt more loved.

"You and me, not so different, eh?" He laughs. "You are growing up so fast. I am happy that we had this talk."

I flash a smile. "So happy you'll give me my phone and computer back?" I push my cheek against his stubbly cheek like I used to when I was a little kid. "Please?"

Dad chuckles. "Okay, I'll give it to you tomorrow. But you cannot turn it on until after your test is finished."

"Of course."

CHAPTER 27

I leave the glistening halls of Winston Academy the same way I always do: with a stomachache.

That SSAT was a beast of a test.

I'm not sure how I did, but I know that I gave it all I had, and that makes me feel pretty darn proud of myself.

With the warm sun shining on my face, I walk through the empty quad and settle onto a shady bench. After pushing my brain to its limit, I want nothing more than to unwind by playing some mind-numbing puzzle games until Yuri comes to pick me up. And now that I have my phone back, I can do just that. Thank goodness!

My phone feels so good in my hands. I'll never take my mobile device for granted again for as long as I live, that's for sure.

I turn it on, and to my surprise, twelve unread text

messages from Felipe and Sienna pop up on my home screen.

> **Felipe:** U ok?
>
> **Sienna:** what happened?
>
> **Sienna:** Let's talk.
>
> **Sienna:** You can call me whenevers. Or text. Or facetime.
>
> **Felipe:** U hanging in there?
>
> **Felipe:** Still haven't heard from you.
>
> **Felipe:** Why weren't you at camp?
>
> **Sienna:** Ur coming to the showcase though, right?
>
> **Felipe:** Didn't see you at the showcase
>
> **Sienna:** It was a great show, would have been better with you there
>
> **Felipe:** You can't stay invisible from us forever, you know.
>
> **Sienna:** Hello?

They're not mad at me?
A weight slides from my shoulders.

This whole time, I'd convinced myself that I was dead to them, but judging from these texts, I was wrong. They were just worried about me.

There's so much I want to tell them.

I facetime Felipe first.

After two rings, his face appears on my screen.

"H-hello?" Seeing him makes me nervous to talk after all this time, after all that's happened.

He smacks his forehead. "Dude, you're alive. Where the heck have you been?"

Before I can reply, a familiar voice calls from the background.

"Hey, is that K—I mean Yumi?"

There's a blur as someone wrestles the phone away from Felipe.

"Sienna?"

"It *is* you!"

"What are you doing at Felipe's?"

"We're practicing for the PAMS audition." She plants herself on a purple couch. "Enough about us. What on earth have *you* been up to? We've been trying to get ahold of you for forever!" She tugs a bright turquoise feather boa away from her neck.

"Sorry." I fidget with my backpack strap. "I was grounded, and my parents took my phone. I only just got it back today."

"I figured you were probably on screen restriction." Sienna rolls her eyes and points her thumb to her side. "Felipe over here thought you were in the witness protection program or got abducted by aliens."

"Completely feasible!" he shouts from the other couch.

I take a deep breath. "Actually, it's great you're together, because I have something to say to you both."

Felipe and Sienna look into the phone, concerned.

"What's up?" Felipe asks.

"I know it was kind of chaotic the last time I saw you. And. Uh. I never got a chance to tell you how sorry I am for lying to you guys. You know, about being Kay."

There's a beat of silence.

"Yeah, I kind of figured it out after the boba shop. I don't know why you wouldn't admit to it. What was up with that, anyway?" Felipe presses.

They listen as I come clean. I don't spare a single detail this time. I even share about how Yuri is moving away, how we're about to lose the restaurant, and how Mom and Dad aren't letting me audition for PAMS.

When I'm done, Felipe's mouth bunches to the side. "Geez, Yumi. I had no idea you were going through so much."

"It all makes sense now," Sienna says. "I feel awful that you had to deal with all that by yourself."

My voice trembles. "No, I'm the one who feels awful. It was totally sucky that I didn't tell you the truth earlier."

Sienna's lip juts out in sympathy. "Aww, Yumi. We forgive you. Right, Felipe?"

"Right," he echoes.

"Don't feel awful anymore, okay?" A sly smile crawls across her lips. "Which reminds me of a joke." She giggles. "What did the chickpea say to his doctor?"

"Huh?"

She makes an exaggerated frowny face. "I falafel." She pauses. "Get it? I feel awful? I falafel?"

"Don't quit your day job, Sienna," Felipe teases, throwing a pillow at her.

She throws it back at him. "Laugh now, but when I'm a famous comedian, you're going to have to pay big bucks to hear my jokes."

I giggle. "Wouldn't it be cool if people really paid us for our jokes? We'd be filthy rich!"

Suddenly, it comes to me. Like a bolt of lightning in the sky.

"Hey, that's it. That's it!" I shout, jumping to my feet.

"What?"

All the dots connect in my mind, and a constellation emerges. "We could tell jokes! To raise money for my family's restaurant!"

"Whaaaaaat?" Sienna tugs at the ends of her feather boa.

"But where? And how?" Felipe's brows knot together.

I'm so psyched, I start pacing back and forth. "We could do a show at our restaurant! Like an open-mic night. Tell jokes or sing or whatever. Maybe we can ask for donations or something. We already have a stage and microphone there. Top-of-the-line sound system, actually."

"Oh! I've always wanted to perform at an open-mic night!" Sienna starts flapping the ends of her boa with excitement. "But instead of asking for donations, you should do a cover charge to enter, like they do at those charity things my parents go to."

"Yes, great idea!" The more I think about it, the more it sounds doable. "The cover charge plus whatever money we earn by selling food and drinks from the regular menu ought to bring in tons of money!"

"Dude, you're going to make bank," Felipe says, nodding thoughtfully. "Whenever we eat Korean barbecue, we go to town. Love that stuff. Especially kalbi, that's my jam. I'm getting hungry just thinking about it."

"We're going to save the restaurant! We're going to save the restaurant!" Sienna sings, her frizzy hair bouncing erratically as she shimmies around Felipe's living room.

"So, who is going to come?" Felipe asks.

"I don't know. I suppose I could reach out to my friends and family," I say.

"Don't you need more people? Maybe you can invite some kids from camp, too." He scrolls through his phone. "I have some of their numbers, and I'm sure they'd want to help out."

"You know what'd be cool? If you could post a flyer on the Haha Club social media account and tag everyone we know!" Sienna suggests.

"Yeah, that'd be the fastest way to spread the word. You should ask Jasmine Jasper for permission to do that," Felipe says.

My tummy flips over at the mention of her name.

"What's wrong?" Felipe asks.

"Well, it's just that I haven't spoken to Jasmine since the day of the showcase dress rehearsal. It's not like I can just waltz into the Haha Club and start asking her for favors."

"It'll give you a chance to talk things over with her," Felipe points out.

"Yeah, it would be great to have some closure. For both of you," Sienna adds.

My fists ball up with anxiety. "But I'm not even sure if she hates me or not . . ."

Sienna shrugs. "I guess you won't know unless you try."

Felipe nods in agreement.

I mull it over. What is holding me back from trying to patch things up with Jasmine? What's the worst that can happen? If I show up and she's unwilling to talk to me, at least I'll know that I tried my best to make things better instead of being a coward and avoiding her for the rest of my life. Deep down, I know I owe her a one-on-one apology and explanation, anyway. I shouldn't let my fear stop me from doing the right thing.

"I'll call you guys back in a bit," I tell my friends.

There's something I need to take care of.

When Yuri drops me off at the Haha Club, I'm bubbling with nerves. The place feels like an empty cave without all the campers. I poke my head inside and spot Jasmine back in the sound booth, fiddling with the equipment.

"Um. Excuse me," I say in a near whisper, approaching her.

She lifts her head up from the dials and knobs on the soundboard, surprised. "Well, hello there, Yumi."

Friendly tone of voice, big smile. No obvious indications that she despises my presence. So far, so good.

I take a step closer.

"What brings you here?" she asks me.

My heartbeat speeds in my chest.

"Er, well, first of all, I wanted to come . . . to . . . um . . . apologize."

I bite my lip.

"I wanted to tell you again how sorry I am for lying to you."

Jasmine cocks her head to side, like she's trying to understand. "I forgive you, Yumi, but I still don't quite understand why you didn't just tell me that you weren't Kay from the beginning. Why'd you drag it out for so long?"

The silence radiates through the room, and it's suddenly very warm.

"I guess at the heart of it, I was afraid that you'd be disappointed. Maybe it was easier for me to go along with things than stand up to set things straight," I say meekly.

Guilt burns like hot sauce on my insides.

"But you taught me that I have to let go of my fears and keep trying, until I have Tutti-Fruitti Jelly Bellies." I stretch my arms open. "So here I am."

The laugh lines around her eyes deepen. "Much respect."

"Which brings me to the other reason I'm here."

She listens intently as I tell her all about my idea to save my family's restaurant.

"I wanted to ask if I you'd be willing to let me post a flyer about our open-mic fund-raiser on the Haha Club website and social media accounts so I can spread the word to all the campers. Maybe they can come out with their families to support us."

She takes a moment to think about it. "I'll do you one better."

Pulling out her phone, she starts tapping through her contacts. "Not only can I post it on the Haha Club, I can also promote it on my local comedy writers group List-serv. Oh, and I have a friend who runs an after-school music program nearby. I can get in touch with her, too."

Jasmine is already thumb texting. "Her students are always looking to perform at open mics."

"But do you think they'll come? Even though they don't know me or my family?"

"Are you joking? Of course! Artists are the biggest backers of small businesses. We know what it's like to hustle. If people get wind that your restaurant is in danger of closing, they'll come out for sure."

A spark of hope rises from within me.

Now I just have to get Mom and Dad on board.

CHAPTER 28

I run the whole way to the restaurant, but it feels more like I'm flying.

"Mom! Dad!" I grab them each by the hand and practically drag them into the back office. "Come quick!"

I wiggle the mouse and pull up the Haha Club website.

"What's going on?" Mom asks as she dries her hands on her apron. "Did they email SSAT exam results?"

"No, but I think I may have figured out how to save the restaurant!" I click to the events page. "We can invite everyone we know to come out for an open-mic fund-raiser show at the restaurant tonight."

"What?" My parents look at me like I'm an alien.

"If people knew that Chung's Barbecue might have to close its doors forever, they would come to support us. We just have to spread the word."

"But how can we contact them?" Dad checks his watch. "Dinner is in five hours."

I turn their attention back to the computer. "With this. It's called a hashtag." I do a quick demonstration of how hashtags and social media work.

"I don't know if this is good idea," Mom says, reserving her judgment. "I don't know what kind of people are going to come from internet."

"It's not like I'm posting it to Craigslist, Mom. Jasmine, the comedy teacher at the camp, said she's willing to promote our event on the Haha Club website and on her vlog. She's got thousands of subscribers. She also said she can invite all her comedian and writer friends in the area. They're all about local businesses staying in the neighborhood."

Mom's forehead wrinkles in surprise. "She said she will help us, after everything that happened?"

I nod. "Yup. Luckily, she really believes in second chances."

"Very wise," Dad says.

Mom stares at the computer screen, puzzled. "You

think the people will come? With only few hours' notice?"

"Only one way to find out."

I twirl my chair to face Dad. "What do you think? We can collect a cover charge and sell food and drinks to raise money."

They still look skeptical.

I push. "Listen, if we want to keep Chung's Barbecue, we need to make six thousand dollars *tonight*. We have no other options. Might as well give it a shot, right? We've got nothing to lose."

My parents look at each other, and my dad breaks into a smile. "Okay. Let's do it! Fighting!"

Mom pulls out her phone. "I will call Manuel and the others to see if they can work tonight."

Out of nowhere, Dad clears his throat. "Maybe I can sing one or two songs, too? It is still my restaurant."

I laugh. "Yes, Dad. Of course."

A short while later, Yuri arrives at the restaurant, still dressed in her Starbucks gear.

"So, what's the emergency? Mom and Dad said something about a show?"

After I explain my vision for the evening, she looks at me strangely, like she's seeing me for the first time.

"Wow, Yooms, that's a genius idea."

I nearly fall out of my chair. Then she asks me, "Tell me, what can I do to help?"

Is my big sister asking little ol' me for direction for the first time ever?

I pass her my clipboard. "Well, I was thinking, since we don't have much time before the event, our main priority is publicity." I flip to the list of all the people we need to invite.

"Can you call everyone here and tell them about our fund-raiser show? I'll work on posting on all the social media platforms. Even Facebook, for the old people."

"Got it. Consider it done." She takes a big breath. "I sure hope this works."

"We won't know until we try, right?"

CHAPTER 29

It's only dusk, and already the atmosphere is buzzing. A steady stream of friends, family, and friends of friends have been arriving since we opened a half hour ago. Yuri and Manuel are in the kitchen cranking out the orders, Dad's back in his suit working the room, Mom's busy giving Mrs. Pak and her family a tour of the place, and I'm running around trying to get everyone seated.

"Jasmine, I'm so glad you're here!" I say when I see her come in.

"Wouldn't miss this for anything." She gives me a big hug. "I want you to meet some friends of mine," she says, introducing me to her former students.

"I really admire what you're doing here," says the guy with the goatee. "It's not easy to survive in this city. It's cool to see you doing something different with your restaurant."

The girl with the long braids looks around the dining room, already shrouded in the aroma of smoky grilled meats. "Totally original concept. K-barbecue and open mic. What a fresh way to bring people together. I'm into it."

"Thanks for coming." I take them to their table, blushing. "I couldn't pull this off without all your help, Jasmine."

"My pleasure, Yumi." She takes a menu. "Now let me see about this kalbi I keep hearing about. Felipe tells me it's going to change my world!"

I ask a waiter to take their order and get back to the business of seating more guests. Then I rush into the kitchen to get what I need to set table five.

"How's it going in here?" I ask.

Yuri grabs a bunch of small porcelain dishes and arranges them onto a platter. "Getting the slam."

Manuel stirs the pots of soup with one hand and throws in the garnish with the other. "But we've got it under control."

"Nice," I say, hoisting the platter onto my shoulder. "I'll deliver this."

On my way out, Manuel yells, "Proud of you, cipota."

I'm all smiles. If someone had told me in the beginning

of the summer that I'd be calling up everyone I know, from besties to acquaintances to near strangers, to invite them to an event I'm throwing, I'd have laughed in their face.

But here we are.

Balancing the platter, I greet some diners I don't recognize at table five. "Hello and welcome to Chung's Barbecue." I pass out the banchan. "Is this your first time dining with us?"

"Yes, it is," says the older gentleman with kind eyes. "Our daughter heard about this place from her comedy camp."

"At the Haha Club?"

"Yes, that's right." He points behind me. "Speak of the devil, there she is. Do you know her?"

I turn my head, and of all people, it's Kay.

I nod. A tremor of nerves shoots through my body, but I don't let it stop me. "Pardon," I say, making my way to her.

"Kay, I'm so glad you could make it!" I call.

To my relief, she recognizes me right away. "Are you kidding? When Sienna and Felipe told me about this, I knew I had to come, too. I missed so much camp because of my dang legs, I thought I'd missed my chance to meet the other kids."

"You're in luck. A lot of them are here tonight. I'll introduce you to everyone after the show."

"Thanks, that'd be so rad."

"So, there's something you should know." I clear my throat. "I'm not sure if anyone explained to you what happened last week. It's kind of a complicated story, but basically, I sort of stole your identity and everyone at camp thought I was you. Look, I'm really sorry—"

"Oh yeah, I know," she says. "Jasmine explained it to us already."

"I still feel really bad about it, and I hope you can forgive me."

"No worries." Her smile is so genuine and sincere that I believe her. "Sounds like it'd make great material for stand-up, actually."

"You're probably right." I smile. "Are you going to perform anything during open mic?"

"I don't know, I'm feeling kind of nervous. It'll be a game-time decision."

"Well, if you decide to, good luck." I point to her legs.

"I'd say break a leg, but it looks like you've already gotten to that. Twice."

We laugh together.

"You're really funny. We should hang out. Maybe watch some Jasmine Jasper videos and do improv."

"Yeah, I'd like that."

We exchange numbers, promising to keep in touch.

I'm headed back to the kitchen when Mom intercepts me in the hallway.

"Yumi, come here." She grabs my arm and pulls me into the office.

"What's up?" I ask impatiently. The place is packed now. "I should get back to help."

"It will just take a minute." She digs through her purse and pulls out her gold pendant necklace. "Here, I want you to wear this. For good luck."

I bite the inside of my cheek.

It's her second-favorite piece of jewelry, after the diamond earrings she sold to pay for my hagwon.

"Mom . . . I don't know what to say."

"Trust me. When you look your best, you will feel your best."

Her warm hands encircle me as she fastens it around my neck.

When she sees it on me, she smiles. "It's big deal to be in the open-mic show. When you go onstage in front of everyone we know, just remember: be calm, don't slouch back, use loud voice, remember to walk around stage, you are not a plant."

Wait, where have I heard that before? I halt when the realization hits me. "Mom, have you been spying on me all those nights I practiced my jokes in my room?"

She plays dumb. "I don't know what you're talking about."

"Mooooom . . ." I smack my forehead. "That was supposed to be private."

"Not so private if I can hear you from the hallway." She clucks her tongue. "If you practiced your mathematics as much as your joke, you would have the PhD!"

Normally I'd fume at the invasion of privacy, but for some reason I don't. She might not understand my passions or agree with all my decisions, but she sees me. As it turns out, she always has.

She tucks my hair behind my ears. "Do a great job tonight."

"Thanks, Mom." I hold the pendant delicately between my fingers. "It's really pretty."

"Like you." She turns away. "Be careful not to lose it. It was very expensive."

I laugh. "I know. I know. I won't."

We are interrupted by a series of earsplitting screeches coming from down the hall.

Mom and I run back to the dining area only to find Dad adjusting the volume dials on the sound board. It screeches one more time before he says, "Hello, I am Mr. Chung. Welcome to our restaurant!" into the mic.

I guess he's eager to start the show. Five minutes ahead of schedule.

"Is everyone having a good time?" he asks.

A cheer rises from the diners.

"Well, I am so happy you can join us on this special night because it is our first time hosting the open mic!"

Mom and I find a seat together in an empty booth toward the back.

"I am very excited." He scratches the back of his

head. "But to tell you truth, I never heard about open mic until my daughter Yumi told me what it is."

Mom elbows me, and I blush at the mention of my name.

"When she told me that anyone can come up to the stage to share talent, any talent, I said great idea! Life is too short to hide the talent. What do you think?"

Applause breaks out across the room.

"He's too good at this," I whisper to Mom, and she nods in agreement.

Dad raises both arms. "That means, ladies and gentlemen, it is time to get show started! Who will be the first performer? Don't be shy!"

A murmur sweeps through the room followed by an almost eerie silence. Someone coughs, and everyone is looking around, but still no one volunteers.

Then I notice the fear creeping into my dad's eyes, just like it did on the night of the Grand Reopening. Something in me snaps. I can't let him go through that again.

Dad jolts a bit when he sees my raised hand.

"Please put hands together for my daughter!" He

points me out in the crowd. "Stand up, Yumi Chung!"

The room thunders with applause, and suddenly the nerves set in.

When I get to the stage, I grip the microphone with both hands. "So, I don't normally do this, but I'm going to share some secret stuff about myself. Stuff I've never shared with anyone in this whole world." My voice wavers into a weird high pitch, and suddenly my confidence falters.

I hesitate.

Do I really have the guts to go through with this?

It's super personal and kind of embarrassing.

A painfully long pause follows.

But then, out of nowhere, I hear Felipe and Sienna chant, "You can do it!" Clap! "You can do it!" Clap-clap! "We believe in Yumi!"

I let out a laugh.

Then they do it again. And this time, everyone in the restaurant joins in, even Mom and Dad. "You can do it!" Clap! "You can do it!" Clap-clap! "We believe in Yumi!"

Jasmine shouts from the back of the restaurant, "Just keep going!"

"Thanks." I regain my footing. "So, you could say I've had a pretty busy summer. You know, going to tutoring, helping out at the restaurant, leading a double life, stealing someone's identity—typical summer for an eleven-year-old."

I look up, and I'm immediately bolstered by the sea of faces from every corner of my life coming together to support me and my family.

"It's true." My voice gets a little louder. "I was an identity thief. The Old Me wasn't cutting it, so I started pretending to be the person I wished I could be. I was convinced that a new haircut or a different name would be all it'd take for me to make friends. Then maybe I wouldn't have to eat lunch by myself in the bathroom anymore."

I wait a beat.

"But now that I think about it, they probably didn't want to be friends with me *because* I was the weird kid who ate lunch by herself in the bathroom."

There's a wave of laughter.

"So my big sister is a genius. Aced the SATs on her first try before she hit her teens. Yeah, not intimidating at all. Did I mention she's also gorgeous? My entire life has been one upstage after another, and to be completely honest, it's hard to hear any advice she has for me. It's no use. I'll never be as perfect as her. She hogged up all the good genes. You know what, though? I think I finally got the last word. The other day she asked me to pass her the lip gloss and I handed her a glue stick . . . and I haven't heard from her since."

Sienna, who is seated between her mom and dad, bursts into giggles. It almost throws me off to see her with her parents, but I keep going.

"How many of you have immigrant parents? Anyone?"

A bunch of people hoot and holler.

"Well, my parents are typical Asian parents. They aren't big on giving compliments. It's a cultural thing. Anyway, the other day we were in the living room hanging out, and I got up to go to bed. I said, 'Good night, Dad!' and then without taking his eyes off the TV, he said, 'I'm proud of you.' I was shocked! I've never heard him say that to me in my whole life. 'What did you say?' I asked him. He pointed to the TV, 'I'm proud of this actor Hugh Jackman. He's best X-men. That Wolverine, waaaaah, so muhshisuh!'

"After that I started growing out my nails, but he still hasn't noticed."

Felipe cracks up the hardest at that one.

"So yeah, as I mentioned, it's been a big summer for me. A lot of wild stuff happened."

I take a deep breath.

"But along the way, I learned that I don't need to become the New Me."

A hush falls over the room.

"Instead, I need to be comfortable being the True Me."

I lock eyes with Mrs. Pak, and she smiles back at me.

"See, I used to let my fear of failure hold me back. From being funny, from putting myself out there in friendships, from telling my parents what's in my heart. I kept comparing myself to other people and trying to be someone I'm not."

Then I turn to face Jasmine again.

"But someone really special taught me that life

isn't about being perfect. I'm starting to see that I'm a work in progress, growing and learning and messing up sometimes. And that's okay. The less I worry about what everyone else is thinking, the more I feel free to be the True Me. And that, my friends, is the secret to why I'm so happy to be up here tonight.

"You all have been great." I take a bow. "I'm Yumi Chung. Thanks for coming to support Chung's Barbecue!" And the place bursts with applause, and I feel like I might just burst myself when people start standing up and cheering for me. Even Manuel and Yuri pop out from the kitchen to join in.

I take another bow and exit the stage, intoxicated by the Comedian's High.

The rest of the open-mic show takes off. The whole time it feels like I'm floating above the room, watching our closest friends gathering around flames of warmth and tasty food, laughing and enjoying each other. And the talent is out of control, too. Ginny reads a moving poem about saving the mangroves, Mr. and Mrs. Lee's son plays Vivaldi on his violin, Jasmine joins a few kids from camp to do some hilarious improv, and Manuel and Sofia sing some Disney Princess songs on karaoke. For the final number, Dad puts on his red-tinted sunglasses and belts out a few of Elton John's greatest hits, which totally brings the house down.

And far too soon, it's time to wrap up our show.

Dad steps up to the mic one last time. "Hope you had a good time. If you liked the meal today and enjoyed the show, please come back again soon."

It isn't until we say goodbye to our guests that I'm hit with a surge of mixed emotions. On one hand, I'm on top of the world. I can't believe we took such a big risk and pulled off an incredible night for our loved ones. Not only that, I finally got to live out my dream of performing comedy for my family, which was beyond incredible.

At the same time, I don't know yet if we made enough money to save the restaurant.

Once everyone has left and the door is locked, it's time to find out.

Dad loosens his necktie. "I am going to check tonight's earnings." He beckons us to join him in the office. "Come with me."

The tension in the room is as thick as abalone porridge as Mom, Yuri, Manuel, and I gather around him in front of the computer.

Dad drums his hands on the desktop and wipes the sweat from his brow.

We lean in close to view the screen.

Dad wiggles the mouse, but then turns to us. "Before I click this, I want to tell you that Chung's Barbecue has been good home for us. For fifteen years, we did a great job serving delicious food and taking care of our customers. Remember that." His voice cracks. "Even if maybe today is our last day here."

He's totally stalling, but that's okay, because I'm not quite ready to find out either.

Manuel puts his hand on Dad's shoulder. "No matter what, it's been a real pleasure, Bong."

Mom's eyes mist over as she pats Manuel on the back. "We are great team." She smiles weakly. "You are the best cook. Even better than me."

"No, no, no." Manuel shakes his head. "Never."

"It's okay, because I taught you."

They share a chuckle.

Yuri sniffs. "I can't imagine my life without this place."

"We must focus on the future now," Dad says quietly.

Hearing that gets me choked up. So much of what's ahead is up in the air. I don't know where I'm going to school for seventh grade, my sister's leaving for the Peace Corps, and we might lose the restaurant. While my heart aches at all the things I'll miss, I take comfort in knowing there's no such thing as failure. Just a chance to pivot and try something different.

"Are you ready?" Dad asks us.

First Yuri grabs my hand and squeezes it. Then I grab Mom's, and Yuri grabs Manuel's. Pretty soon we're in a huddle around Dad.

"Yes," we say together.

We brace ourselves.

It's the moment of truth.

Dad clicks the button, and we all hold our breath.

The site takes forever to load, but then it comes up.

$7,214.31

For a second, no one reacts.

"Is this real?" I whisper.

Mom hesitates. She nudges my sister. "Yuri, double-check it."

Yuri grabs a pen and starts scribbling calculations on the notepad. She looks up, smiling. "Yes, according to my calculations this figure is correct. Which means, ladies and gentlemen, Chung's Barbecue will live to see another day!"

"Holy Hot Cheetos!" I scream.

Pandemonium breaks out, and we're all screaming and hugging and jumping and hugging some more. The commotion is so loud, it's like New Year's Day and Christmas and the Fourth of July combined!

Dad grabs Manuel's hand and gives it a vigorous shake.

"We did it! We did it!"

Mom strokes the top of my head, then cups my cheeks. "Because of your brave idea, Yumi."

Dad pulls me into a hug. "We are so proud of you."

"Prouder than you were of Hugh Jackman?"

Everyone laughs, and tears of joy drip down my face.

CHAPTER 30

A week later, I'm crying for another reason.

A dry summer breeze gusts by as Yuri and I stand around the driveway waiting for Dad to finish loading her bags into the trunk.

"Why did you have to choose Nepal? It's so far." I bite my lip, and I blink back tears. "Do you really have to leave?"

"I'm afraid so, Yooms."

Yuri puts her arm around my shoulder. "Don't worry, I'll be back for a visit soon enough. Anyway, you're going to be so busy with school and improv classes." She gives me a little nudge.

I can't help but crack a smile. After the open-mic show, my sister somehow persuaded Mom and Dad to let me take Saturday classes at the Haha Club on the condition I get straight As. "Thanks for making that happen, by the way."

"Don't mention it." She winks. "I can tell already, you're going to have such a great time, you won't even miss me."

I sigh. For someone with her IQ, she couldn't be more wrong. I'm going to miss her every single day, every single hour. "You better email me."

She crosses her heart. "Every time I have Wi-Fi, I promise," she says with a smile.

While the thought of navigating the world without my big sister makes me want to superglue myself to her side before she gets on that plane, I know she needs this. Already, her face looks fuller and glowier than it has in a long time. But that doesn't make it any easier for me to say goodbye.

From my pocket, I hand her a tiny box wrapped in colorful paper. "This is for you. For good luck."

Yuri brightens in surprise. "What's this? You didn't have to get me anything!"

"It's nothing. Really."

I look over her shoulder as she carefully opens the itty-bitty box. She covers her mouth with both hands and laughs. Inside, in one corner, on top of pink tissue paper, is the scraggle of black thread Yuri mistook for a spider that day in the garage. I took the liberty of gluing on googly eyes and a bow tie.

"I thought it'd help you overcome your fears," I offer.

"Thanks, Yooms." She hugs me. "I'm sure I'll be needing this little guy. A lot."

Suddenly, Mom comes running from the house with a thick fleece jacket.

"Don't forget this!" She drapes it over my sister's shoulders like a blanket.

Yuri folds it over her arm. "Mom, honestly! It's over ninety degrees today!"

"It's always cold on the plane." She stashes a Ziploc bag of seaweed rice rolls in the jacket pocket. "Kimbap, so you don't get hungry. Food on airplane is no good."

Dad finally slams the trunk closed and hollers, "Okay, all packed up. We should go. Before traffic gets bad." His eyes are glassy, and he looks down at his shoes. He's as bad with goodbyes as I am.

To break the sadness, I ask, "Why don't we get one last family selfie in front of the house before we head out?"

"Good idea!" Dad says, subtly wiping the side of his face with a sleeve.

I hold up my phone with an outstretched arm, and we crowd together behind it.

"One! Two! Three!" Dad yells, "Say 'kimchi'!" We smile and pose holding up our fingers in peace signs.

Click!

When I hold the screen close to get a good look at it, my knees almost buckle and the blood drains from my face.

"What's the matter?" Yuri asks.

"It's an email." My heart thuds in my chest. "From the Secondary School Admission Test Committee."

"Your test results came?" Mom says, craning her neck to see.

I swallow hard. "I guess."

"Open it!" Mom and Dad say at the same time.

With trembling hands, I reach to tap open my email, but then Mom grabs the phone from me before I get a chance to see my score.

I brace myself for the outcome—it could go either way.

I'll just have to roll with it, no matter what happens.

Her eyes bounce left and right as she reads the words on the screen.

She lets out a squeal. "Yumi, you got the scholarship!"

"Wah!" Dad grabs my shoulders and squeezes. "Isn't this great?"

I don't say anything, because there's a whole tangle of thoughts piling up in my brain.

"Yumi, how do you feel?" Yuri grabs my hands in hers.

"Are you okay with this?" Mom looks to me for my reaction.

They listen, waiting to hear what I have to say.

I stand there on the driveway collecting my thoughts, surrounded by the fierce love of my family.

"You know"—I finally speak—"I never thought I'd say this, but I'm fine with it."

Even I'm surprised that Winston no longer scares me. After scheming the entire summer to get out of returning, I realize that it wasn't Winston itself that was holding me back. It was my fear of it. I imagine myself walking through Winston's halls, and I know this year will be different because I'm not the same person I was last year. I'm ready to be heard. And I don't need to go to a new school for that, because no matter where I go, I'm still going to get my new beginning, my fresh start.

As the True Me.

ACKNOWLEDGMENTS

When I set out to write a book, I had no idea of all that went into it. Luckily, I had a team of talented people alongside me to help bring Yumi's story to you.

To Joanna Cárdenas, my editor and fellow comedy nerd, I knew from our first conversation that you *got* this story, and this book would not be what it is without your unending patience, fierce support, and eagle eye. A big shout-out to the whole team at Kokila for all your feedback and love.

To everyone at Penguin Random House, what can I say but WOW. I couldn't have asked for a better debut experience. I'm so proud to publish with you.

To Thao Le, my agent extraordinaire, I'm so happy to have snagged you. Working with you has confirmed my suspicion that when Asian ladies team up, there's nothing we can't do.

To Quincy Cho and René Colato Laínez, thank you for your invaluable insight.

Thank you, Susanna Spies, for volunteering your time to talk to me about the ins and outs of comedy camp and all the zaniness that ensues there.

To Jennifer Hom, thank you for your work on the cover art.

To Beth Phelan, who organizes #DVpit, keep doing what you're doing; it's changing lives!

To my AMMFAM, it's been a gift to journey through this road to publication with you all. Special thanks to Adrienne Kisner, Alyssa Colman, and Julie Abe for all the perfectly chosen GIFs, good advice, and friendship.

To my SCBWI San Diego critique group: Danielle, Jeanne, Ruth, Alyssa, and Carol, you've read every draft, from when Yumi was on a bus making jokes about dogs as backpacks to now. When I first joined this group, I was hesitant to tell anyone I was a writer, but you all pushed me to be bold in my craft, ignore the rejections, and keep dreaming. Thank you, for everything.

To Kellie, plot doctor and dear friend. Our bimonthly meetings at the French Café have been the breeding grounds for many of my best ideas, thanks to you and your ingenious suggestions—truly, your fingerprints are all over this book.

To the Kimchingoos, the best writing sisters a girl could ask for! Susan, Graci, Grace, and Sarah, we may be scattered all around the world, but you're so near and dear in my heart. I am stronger because of you. Nube putchears forever!

A great big thank you to my NYC sisters: Julie, Wenny, Nancy, and Jeannie. You were the first to encourage me to write a book way back when we were raising babies. Thank you for believing in me before I believed in myself.

To my besties, Gower, Sylvia, Charlene, Christina, Isabel, Julie, Jamie: our annual girls' trip spurs me to be a better version of myself because I'm so inspired by you all.

Special thanks to my 가족, who always have my back: Mos, Mari, John, Joshua, Sophia, Emma, Emily, Audrey, Sharon, Oscar, Susanna, Mike, Baby Joshua, 아버님, and 어머님.

To my sisters, Heidi (미라) and Lillian, who are my

biggest fans but also the first to tell me when my shoes are ugly, which is often. #widefeetproblems. Thank you for keeping me grounded and uplifted at the same time.

To 엄마 (and all immigrant parents everywhere): thank you for your many sacrifices and all your hard work in raising us. We can rise only because we stand on your shoulders.

To my daughters, Olivia and Lily, this book is for you. The things I always tell you are in this book: do your very best in all things, study hard, clean your room, eat a lot, and follow your heart!

To Phil, who is the very best. We did it!